THE SATANIC RITES OF SASQUATCH AND OTHER WEIRD STORIES

NICK CATO

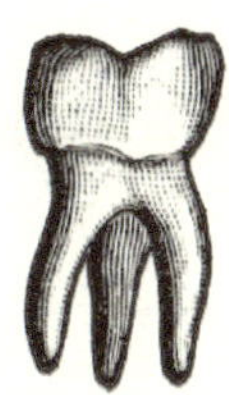

WHAT WAS CALLED
(Originally appeared in *Dark Fusions: Where Monsters Lurk!* 2013 PS Publishing)

KILLING BY THE MOON
(Previously unpublished)

WHISKER WHIPPED
(Originally appeared in *Hamsters! A Fabulous Anthology* (For Fabulous Raye), 2014 Dynatox Ministries)

ANTIBACTERIAL POPE
(Originally appeared at *Southern Fried Weirdness Online*, 2007)

THE SATANIC RITES OF SASQUATCH
(Previously unpublished)

THE AIRCRASH BUREAU
(Originally appeared in *Houdini Gut Punch*, 2010 Library of Bizarro Horror Press)

INSIDE THE JIGGLES CAFÉ
(Previously unpublished)

THE HUSBAND
(Previously unpublished)

I BURIED A FERGASON
(Originally appeared in *Southern Fried Weirdness*, 2007 Southern Fried Weirdness Press)

SHOP 'TILL YOU DROP
(Originally appeared in *Christmas in Hell*, 2012 Drunken Skald Press)

ANARCHY CAFÉ
(Originally appeared in *Blood for You: A Literary Tribute to GG Allin*, 2015 Weirdpunk Books)

THE BOWL
(Previously unpublished)

HERS IS A LUSH SITUATION
(Originally appeared in *50 Secret Tales of the Whispering Gash: A Queefrotica*, 2013 CreateSpace)

THE LIFE MACHNE
(Originally appeared in *Strange Stories of Sand and Sea*, 2008 Fine Tooth Press)

Published by Bizarro Pulp Press
an imprint of Journal Stone
www.bizarropulppress.com

Cover Design by Mikio Murakami
Interior Design by Jess Landry

ISBN (sc): 978-1-947654-85-3
ISBN (ebook): 978-1-947654-86-0

Printed in the USA.

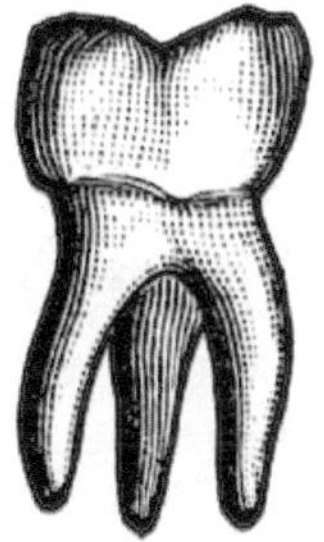

THE SATANIC RITES OF SASQUATCH AND OTHER WEIRD STORIES

WHAT WAS CALLED

KILLING BY THE MOON

WHISKER WHIPPED

ANTIBACTERIAL POPE

THE SATANIC RITES OF SASQUATCH

THE AIRCRASH BUREAU

INSIDE THE JIGGLES CAFÉ

THE HUSBAND

I BURIED A FERGASON

SHOP 'TIL YOU DROP

ANARCHY CAFÉ

THE BOWL

HERS IS A LUSH SITUATION

THE LIFE MACHINE

WHAT WAS CALLED

Author's Note: I was thrilled to sell this story to an editor I admire quite a bit, and also to be part of a PS Publishing anthology. A lot of my "serious" horror stories deal with religion, so it was great to bring that into the Lovecraftian universe. This is one of my personal favorites.

October 14, 2011

Everything seemed much brighter than it did on television, including the detective's attitude. While he wasn't in a joking or time-wasting mood, Father Frank Millsen couldn't see him raising his voice or using threats to pull information that might not be there.

"Have you seen the coroner's report?"

Father Millsen shook his head *no*.

Detective Samuel Hindes slid a manila envelope across the table. "Take your time."

The 27-year-old Catholic priest scanned several pages of text that had apparently been done on an old-fashioned typewriter. When he came to the autopsy photos—which included a pre-autopsy X-ray shot—a slight layer of sweat began forming on his forehead. Detective Hindes pretended to focus on the photos, but Father Millsen knew he was waiting for some kind of off-key reaction.

The priest shook his head for nearly two minutes as he looked over the graphic pictures.

"So." Detective Hindes placed a toothpick between his lips. "Is there anything you can tell me that might shed some light on this?"

Father Millsen stared at the silhouette of the X-ray picture despite the clear and undeniable proof of the autopsy shots.

"You *are* the priest who administered Communion to the victim, Timothy Connor, on Sunday, October eleventh, are you not?"

"Yes, I am."

"And you claim you're one hundred percent certain you placed an ordinary Communion wafer into the victim's mouth?"

"Detective, can you *please* stop referring to the parishioner as 'the victim'? He wasn't a victim, but a faithful worshipper."

"No offense intended, Father." The detective slid the toothpick across his lips, then folded his hands on the table. His shoulders now looked as broad as a linebacker's. "But the person in these photos is now deceased, and according to this report, it's the thing lodged in his throat that killed him. That makes him a victim."

Father Millsen looked over the pictures, wondering how mentally strong coroners must be to slice open cadavers as routinely as priests lit candles in the sanctuary. Then he thought of Timothy Connor, the 46-year-old widowed father of three daughters, who'd lost his life three days ago, less than a minute after receiving Holy Communion...the very first Communion Millsen had given to anyone.

* * *

August 21, 2001

He was really doing it. After years of his grandmother's encouragement, and with the blessing of his mother, Frank Millsen was now on his way to his first year of seminary.

"Are you sure this is what you want?" his father had asked the previous night as Frank packed his suitcase. "It's not too late to change your mind."

But Frank was convinced with all his heart that this was God's calling. He never found church to be the dull, lifeless place that his friends and most of his family bemoaned. He'd never doubted the existence of God or the authority of the church, and since he could remember, he had always enjoyed attending Mass and his early years of service as an altar boy.

"If this is what you really want, go for it," his mother had said a few days after his high school graduation. "I know your grandmother's gonna be thrilled."

Frank watched the buildings of New York City turn to trees as he headed north to Saint John Seminary in Connecticut. There were only five other people on the bus, giving him plenty of quiet in which to contemplate his future...and to try and remember exactly what had transpired just over a month ago at his friend's beach house in Long Island.

* * *

July 1, 2001

Frank's friends had finally accepted the fact that he wasn't joking about joining the priesthood. And they finally agreed they wouldn't have a prostitute or a sympathetic ex-girlfriend waiting for him at Danny's parents' summer home in the Hamptons. They were all meeting there for one last week together before Frank went off to seminary and they went to college and trade school. Not that Frank had many girlfriends; there had been Mary Wagner in the 8th grade, with whom he'd seen a couple movies and kissed a few times before realizing he didn't have any interest. And while he'd gone out with Kelly McHugh for almost three months during their sophomore year, she grew tired of him not "making a move" and eventually stopped calling.

Both girls had laughed each time he'd invited them to Mass, which he found funny, since they were both Catholic. But as his surprised grandmother told him when he began to show interest, few people these days were serious about God.

"Snap out of it, Padre!" Danny slapped the back of his head as they sped out of Queens on the Belt Parkway. "This is your LAST chance to have fun before the Big Guy upstairs takes you away from us."

Frank laughed, gave Danny a high five to let him know he was still with them, then turned and stuck his tongue out at Kevin and Mike, which earned him two more slaps to the head.

He was looking forward to a few days stretched out on the private beach, perhaps taking in the sun for the last time in who knew how long.

They wasted no time putting their things away as soon as they arrived. Danny was already on the phone ordering a couple pizzas. He mentioned that for the rest of the week they'd take turns cooking on the grill.

They sat on the back deck after dinner, watching the sun descend over the spotless beach. Frank found it amazing how beautiful the shore was here, just a short drive from the less than clean beaches around the city.

Danny, Kevin and Mike sipped bottles of beer while Frank stuck with his Snapple Peach iced tea.

"You mean you're not even gonna have *one* drink? I mean, this is your last couple weeks of freedom," Mike said, putting his feet up on the fence surrounding the deck.

"One beer and you're already starting to break my chops?"

Mike gave an apologetic look, then cracked open a second beer. "Okay, okay...suit yourself."

"Thank you."

Danny stood up. Looking at the darkening horizon, he said, "I gotta hand it to you, Frank. No booze. No girls. What do you—"

"Come on, guys. Let's just hang and relax. I told you a thousand times: I'm not gay, I don't need girls, and I'm fine with my Snapple—which I'll still be allowed to have even when I become a priest. Besides, you know I was never a big drinker."

Frank's buddies laughed.

"Oooh! Sign me up!" Kevin said as he took his shirt off. Frank flung his bottle cap at him as he walked off the deck. "But in the meantime, I'm going to take a dip. Anyone coming?"

When everyone shook their heads *no*, Kevin downed the rest of his beer and made his way to the surf. "See ya's in a few."

He dove into the ocean headfirst, then waded around close to shore. Frank was considering joining him when something caught his attention off to the right. "The neighbors up to something?"

Danny tried to see what was going on, but the darkness made it difficult. He went inside and came out a minute later with binoculars. He scanned the beach and whistled.

"How can you see anything? It's so dark out," Mike said.

"Night vision, baby. But none of you are using this—if it breaks, my old man will kick my ass."

"What's going on over there?"

"Looks like a nice little party," Danny said. "And it looks like Kev's heading there without us." He put the goggles back in their case, then yelled, "Wait up!"

Kevin waved and slowed his pace.

Danny and Mike grabbed Frank by the arms and pulled him up. "Come on. You're coming—or we'll de-pants you and drop you off at the supermarket."

Frank shrugged his friends' arms off. "Relax. I'm coming."

As they walked down the beach, Danny noticed a small fire had been lit. There seemed to be about a dozen people dancing around it, the music growing louder as they approached.

"Do you know anyone around here?" Frank asked.

"Of course. This is probably Mindy and her friends. They always have a party going when her parents are away," Danny said.

Wonderful, Frank thought, wanting to turn back. But he knew it'd just bring ridicule, so he figured he'd go along with things and see what was what.

* * *

"Hey. Are you okay?"

Frank felt something wet on his face and his feet. The incoming tide licked at his saturated sneakers, and he realized a dog was licking his chin as soon as his eyes opened. Its owner tugged the Great Dane back on its leash. "Stop that, Blaze!"

"It's okay," Frank said as he sat up. It took a few moments, but he realized where he was.

"Big party last night?" the old man asked.

"Must've been."

The old man laughed. "You kids should take it easy...especially around the ocean."

"I'll remember that. Thank you."

The man nodded and walked on, Blaze a few paces ahead. Frank stood up and felt a bit dizzy, despite his sobriety. The fire that had served as the party's center was now a simple hole, and someone had taken the time to clean up; there were no beer bottles, cans, or any kind of garbage as far as he could see.

He wondered why his friends had left him on the sand, so close to the water, and began to head back to Danny's house.

Frank had been drunk several times before, but had never taken drugs—not even a hit off a joint. He wondered if someone had spiked his Snapple—images came and went through his mind with every other step he took through the tiring sand.

-Girls dancing without their bikini tops.

-Danny walking off with one of them shortly after they joined the party.

-One of the guys psycho-babbling about the ocean and the history of the area.

-The ocean glowing orange.

-The music slowing down and speeding up.

-The ocean and sky meshing into one.

Frank was winded by the time he reached Danny's deck, the sun already strong. He caught his breath and checked his watch: 7:42 a.m.

"Come on—open up." Frank pounded on the frame of the glass doors leading to the kitchen. "Real nice of you morons to cut out on me last night."

When no response came, he walked to the front door, intending to let his anger out on the doorbell, but that was when he noticed Danny's car was gone. It was also the first time Frank regretted not having a cell phone.

He walked down to Mindy's house to see if they were there; if not, he would ask to use her phone.

"Mindy? Mindy's not back from school for another week," an older woman said, presumably Mindy's mother.

Frank paused. The image of robed people dancing around a fire flooded his brain, then left as quickly as it had arrived.

"Are you okay, young man?"

"Y-yes. Sorry—it seems my friends left me here," Frank said, not wanting to add to the weirdness of the situation. "I'm locked out of Danny's house. I think he ran to the store or something. Do you think I could use your phone to call him?"

"Danny Driscoll?"

"Yes. We're up here for the week."

"Sure—I'll be right back," the woman said. She returned quickly with a cordless phone and handed it to him, keeping the door half-closed.

"Thank you." Frank dialed Danny's cell number. Danny picked up on the fourth ring.

"Where are you guys?" Frank asked.

"Frank?"

"Yes, it's Frank. Why did you guys leave me on the beach last night?"

After a brief pause, Danny said, "What are you talking about, brother? What beach?"

"Listen, man, I'm not in the mood for this. My legs are soaking wet and I'm locked out of your house. Are you guys at the store or something?"

"Dude, I'm sitting on my front stairs."

"What are you talking about? I'm in front of Mindy's house right now—"

"Mindy's house? Long Island Mindy?"

"Yes, Long Island Mindy—unless there's another one you haven't told me about."

"It sounds like *you're* busting *my* chops now. I'm in Queens."

Frank dropped his arm and stared at Mindy's mother. The woman closed the door a bit more.

Danny's voice asked, "Hello? You still there?"

Frank handed the phone back and said, "Thank you. They'll be back in a few minutes."

He headed back to Danny's house as more images revealed themselves.

-Two men forcing him to his knees by the surf.

-Naked Mindy rubbing herself on him and slithering around him as he knelt.

-The partiers screaming and applauding as the sky turned red.

***

July 11th, 2001

Frank Millsen woke up on the beach by Mindy's house for the second time in less than two weeks. This time, not only did he know his friends hadn't come with him, but he had no recollection of how he'd gotten there.

He stood up and looked over the ocean, expecting similar images to those of his first "blackout" to begin attacking his mind. He walked back toward Danny's house, hoping one of his parents was there; otherwise he'd need to take public transportation home.

While his mind remained clear of obscure images, a sense of *calling* came over him; a sense that something on this beach or in the nearby ocean had required his presence.

Unlike last time, Frank had woken up far enough away from the surf that his legs remained dry. But it didn't make the trek across the sand any less tiring.

* * *

April 21, 2003

Saint John Seminary, Connecticut

While Frank Millsen had excelled in every theology course, he found himself struggling with the current lessons on transubstantiation; more specifically, he struggled with the idea that he would be commissioned to say a prayer over a Communion wafer, turn its *essence* into the body of Christ, and deliver that body to Christ's followers. He understood there'd be no visible physical change to the wafer—he'd believed this fact since he was a kid. But he got jitters from the idea that he, as a mere mortal, would have the ability to perform this miracle simply because the Church was ordaining him.

Will I really have the power to do this? Will I really be able to call God down from heaven whenever I say Mass?

He slid his notebook across his dorm room's small desk and put his head down. Where was this doubt coming from? Why had he never thought of this before? Was this God testing his faith, or Satan trying to undermine his last two years of study?

***

October 14, 2011

Father Frank Millsen reluctantly agreed to tell Detective Hindes his story, but Hindes wanted to know his background before he had become a priest. Frank explained how he'd never been one for drugs or alcohol, how he'd always been the rational thinker among his friends when they hit their teenage years, and how he'd discovered his interest in God at an uncommonly young age.

"So you mean to tell me you've lived *that* straight a life? No partying? No sex? No nothing?"

"I've been to plenty of parties, but never cared for drinking. I was the one who made sure everyone got home safe."

The detective rolled his eyes. "So basically you're telling me you've never been in trouble, have never been in a situation where..."

Father Millsen thought about the beach thing back in the summer of 2001, and wondered if it was something the detective might find useful. He told the story, but couldn't tell what the cop was thinking. When he was finished, Hindes leaned back on his chair and popped a fresh toothpick into his mouth.

"So you mean to tell me you found yourself in Long Island, thinking your friends were with you, only to discover there was no party, no week-long getaway, and your friends said they hadn't been there with you for a single second?"

"Yes." Father Millsen kept eye contact.

"And you're serious that you hadn't been on any kind of drugs or alcohol?"

"I'm serious. Mindy's father was even nice enough to give me a ride back to Queens the second time it happened. To this day my friends think I made the whole story up. Either that, or they figure it was some kind of delusional panic attack that hit when I realized I was giving up a 'normal' life for the priesthood. But I've known for a long time this is what I wanted to do, so there were never any doubts or panic. Even the other priests at my parish don't know how to explain what happened to me throughout those two days."

Father Millsen was surprised when the detective quickly stood up and walked over to a lone file cabinet. He pulled out an envelope and sat back down at the table. "There's one more thing I'd like you to tell me."

He handed Millsen a clear plastic bag. Inside was a Communion wafer; only, unlike a common wafer, this one had several white strands sticking out from each side.

"Is this the wafer you placed in Timothy Connor's mouth?"

Millsen studied the bag for a few moments, then said, "No it's not, Detective. I already told you I gave him the same wafer that's administered to millions of people every day during every Mass. I've never seen one like this before in my life."

* * *

November 1, 2011

Detective Hindes had sat outside Frank Millsen's rectory every night since the interrogation. His partner Dave thought he was crazy for doing all this extra leg work, considering the priest's spotless record. But Hindes was convinced something else was going on—either an Academy Award-worthy performance from an off-balanced priest, or something the priest himself wasn't aware of—

Detective Hindes' cell phone rang, startling him from his thoughts.

"Sam, are you at the rectory again?" Detective Dave Washington asked.

"Yep. What are you doing up so late?"

"I was just informed that a couple of uniforms over in Bayside responded to a call at the Saint Raymond New Cemetery. Turns out someone exhumed the body of Tim Connor about three hours ago...

and it's nowhere to be found. I'm heading over now."

"I'll meet you there in ten minutes."

Just as Detective Hindes turned the key in the ignition, Father Millsen walked out the rectory's front door and slid into a car parked in the adjacent lot. Hindes called his partner back.

"Looks like Father Spotless is on the move. I'm on him. Give me a call if you find anything out at the cemetery."

"Gotcha."

* * *

Detective Hindes followed the priest to the end of the Belt Parkway, then all the way across Long Island on the Southern State; he was more than happy that he'd filled up his tank before tonight's stakeout.

Frank Millsen finally parked in front of a gorgeous two-story home somewhere in the Hamptons. Hindes parked at the end of the block and watched Millsen get out of the car and walk around the side of the house.

Hindes caught up to the priest, but kept back a good hundred yards. Although Hindes hadn't seen the priest walk much outside of leaving the interrogation room, Millsen seemed to be in some kind of trance—or, more than likely, he knew he was being followed and was putting on an act.

Millsen made his way down the shoreline, his black vestments making him nearly invisible. Hindes had nowhere to hide, but crept along low, hoping not to alert the priest; he *had* to see where this guy was headed.

A fire came into view, causing Millsen's figure to stand out against an otherwise pitch-black sky, and as Hindes came closer, he remembered the priest's testimony: the fire, people dancing around in robes—just about everything Millsen had described in his story two weeks ago seemed to be happening again.

Hindes could hear everything going on, and he chanced creeping a little closer to see some details. One of the robed people put his hands on the back of Millsen's shoulders and walked him toward the surf. The others stopped dancing and followed. A body lay by the water, its neck ripped open. A trail of blood and gore came from the gash and led to the water; the slight moonlight seemed to exist just to make the trail visible. Even in the darkness, Hindes knew it was the body of Timothy Connor.

"You have completed your work, Brother Frank. You have completed your calling, Father Millsen."

Hindes' first instinct was to run over and put an end to whatever this little gathering was; surely these freaks were responsible for Timothy's grave robbery and most likely—somehow—his death. But he listened as the robed leader called for everyone to face the ocean. Robes dropped. Thirteen naked people stood at full attention. The leader turned to face them, his back to the sea. He pushed Father Millsen down to his knees and continued.

"We have waited for this day for far too long. We have prayed for the Great One's coming since we were children, as did our parents and grandparents before us."

The group raised their hands. Hindes noticed some of them crying as he crept closer with his semi-automatic drawn.

Timothy Connor's neck sealed itself up. Something that Hindes thought looked like a long strand of seaweed pulled the corpse into the ocean. The ocean began to turn orange, then red. When it began bubbling, the naked worshippers began to dance around the priest, kissing him, hugging him. Father Millsen looked straight ahead, indifferent to the dramatic changes going on around him.

Hindes thought the sea looked like a giant pot of boiling water. The worshippers picked up the priest and backed away, still looking at the ocean as something slowly rose from about two hundred feet out.

"Welcome! Welcome!" the leader said. As if on cue, his followers raised the priest in the air and walked back to the surf as the thing stood, easily sixty feet tall.

Hindes ran back, slapping himself on the cheek to try and catch his breath. The monstrosity towered with a head full of eyes, its body covered in lumps, seaweed, and white gunk, several arms of various lengths flapping about in every direction. One of the stretchy arms snatched the priest—and the person who'd been closest to the surf—and tossed both into its massive maw, swallowing them with seemingly no effort. The thing's body began to shed the seaweed, and its pure-white skin glowed with fury, causing the worshippers and Detective Hindes to shield their eyes as it took its first step onto the beach.

One by one, the naked worshippers offered themselves to the squid-like beast. Its body grew taller and wider with each body it consumed, each eye projecting a satisfied, appreciative look.

Hindes made it back to his car as the first home on the exclusive block was smashed to pieces; the creature flattened it with one step off the sand and into civilization—into its new kingdom.

* * *

October 13, 2011

The coroner looked over the x-rays as soon as they came in from St. Vincent's Hospital. Timothy Connor's body was laid out before him, and he had the go-ahead to perform the autopsy.

When Connor's neck was opened and pinned back for examination, he could see the alleged communion wafer. It looked the same as any normal wafer, albeit with several small strands protruding from each side. The strands had apparently caused the wafer to lodge in the victim's throat.

The coroner gently poked the wafer with a scalpel. He jumped back when the strands wrapped themselves around the surgical tool and then quickly retracted.

With a pair of long surgical pliers, he pulled the wafer from the victim's throat and placed it in a plastic container. He quickly twisted the lid closed, expecting the wafer to crawl around like a captured spider, but it lay motionless.

After waiting a few minutes, he removed the wafer and placed it on a steel tray under a bright examination light. He poked and pulled at it, attempting to get a similar reaction as with his initial prod, but it remained still. It had a heavy, fleshy consistency, not a standard wafer's lightweight texture.

Had he imagined the strands lunging at his scalpel? Had this most unusual case put him on edge?

The coroner removed the wafer from the exam tray and placed it in a clear evidence bag. A detective would be coming for it soon. The coroner looked forward to examining the wafer more closely when he returned the next day.

He started pressing the bag's lips together, but before he could seal it, the wafer leapt out and attached itself to his mouth. He wanted to scream but couldn't. He staggered back as the strands wiggled their way inside his mouth. One tendril pricked the tip of his tongue. Desperately he clawed at his mouth, trying to wrench it open, but his jaw was locked shut.

Seconds later, he heard a voice.

When I am returned from blessing the one who called me, you will place me back from where you took me.

The coroner felt a jolt of excruciating pain as he looked over at the hole in Timothy Conner's neck. The voice added, *Do you understand?*

As soon as he mumbled "Mmm-hmmm," the agony stopped. The wafer detached itself and fell back into the evidence bag.

Relieved and suddenly dizzy, the coroner sealed the bag and stepped away, collecting himself.

KILLING BY THE MOON

Author's Note: One of my best friends is a biker. Most bikers I know are cool people, more interested in helping others than causing trouble. I always wondered what set some bikers off, so I threw a nice guy (partially based on my friend) into an absurd situation.

My first couple of murders were very annoying. The next batch, while still uncomfortable, became a bit easier. Today, eight months since I began my spree, I've got this down to a science. As you *might* be able to understand, my technique requires much humility, and at times, a suspension of belief...even for myself. But for someone who has a retractable belly-knife permanently imbedded in his ass, I've quickly become one of the more notorious serial killers in American history, and it all started with a stupid prank.

My friend Harry always throws crazy parties, especially on New Year's Eve. Until things went haywire, this year's bash was going great. The music was blasting, the booze flowing, and Harry's Lower East Side apartment held a capacity crowd. I can't remember if it was me, Harry, or the redhead I'd been groping all night, but a bunch of us decided it'd be funny if we streaked over to a deli to pick up some more beer. Yeah, this was a dumb idea for a bunch of forty-somethings to consider, but the combination of Heineken and Aerosmith must've put some of us into high-school mode.

Everyone at the party cracked up as we left Harry's place, taking the stairs for maximum exposure. We ran down Avenue A, all of us guys covering our shrinkage (remember, this was January 1st in New York City). Caroline (my redheaded flirt-buddy) kept her pants on, but her naturally bouncy melons caused several cars to skid to screeching halts.

When we entered some bodega three blocks away, I knew the cashier didn't want our business. I made sure he saw the money in my hand, but it was no use.

"Out! All of you! Out of here! Come back with clothes!"

Caroline and some other guy put four cases of Budweiser on the counter. I remember saying, "We're leaving—just take this and keep the change," when the clerk jumped over our brew and showed us an unopened knife.

I gotta give this guy credit. He had some real guts. It's not every bodega owner who's willing to stand up to a bunch of naked, drunken biker-types.

"Out! Or I call police!"

"Just take it easy, Mr. Pac Man," I said, figuring he wouldn't understand my insult to his native country.

"Pac Man? PAC MAN?"

Before I knew what had happened, my face hit the floor, and I saw Caroline leading everyone out with the beers. Apparently I ticked this guy off enough for him to lay me out like a school girl (and I'm six foot one, two hundred and twenty pounds).

My world changed when I tried to get up. The owner was screaming something in his native language when I reached around his arm. The knife handle must have flipped in his hand. As he strived to jab me in the back, I felt something cold and hard enter my rectum. I knew I'd been stabbed in the ass.

But it wasn't a sharp pain. I was thankful, realizing the knife never opened. I imagined this was what it felt like to be raped in prison. Angered and embarrassed, I turned and took a swing, but he was too fast for me in my drunken state; he ducked with plenty of time to spare. I tried to pull out the knife, but it was jammed in real nice.

I dove on top of him, sitting on his chest, punching his face repeatedly. The sucker was tough. He managed to crack me in the jaw with his right fist, which in turn sent my rage into overdrive, and that's when I felt a *click* underneath me. I saw his eyes widen. Warm liquid hit my thighs. I stood up as soon as he went limp.

There was a slit in his chest, which continued to pump out blood. Perhaps the blade had reached his heart. I ran to the back of the store, felt between my legs, and squirmed. The blade sticking out of me must have been six or seven inches long. What was I supposed to do now?

"Andy!" I heard Caroline calling me. "Where are you?"

Out of instinct, I clenched my butt cheeks, and the blade withdrew with a muffled *click*. I felt it to verify, and yeah, the blade was back in its handle.

Which was *in me*.

Caroline had run back to Harry's for our clothes. She used my shirt to dab the blood off me as I carefully slid into my jeans.

"We'd better get you to a hospital," she said.

"No! I'm okay! Most of the blood is his," I said, happy to see this didn't upset her.

"We'd best get out of here."

As we ran past the clerk's body, I could tell he was history.

I had killed him.

And I knew I'd found the coolest girl on earth when we went back to Caroline's place and had sex for over three hours. Each time I climaxed, I worried the blade would shoot out and cut her leg or arm, but it didn't. And not once did she bring up the fact that I'd just killed someone.

Bikers are like that...at least, those of us who come from the old school. We seem to keep a stronger code of silence than the Mafia.

Eight months after becoming a human belly-knife (or, should I say, *ass-knife*), I'm still amazed that none of my friends have asked me if I was responsible for the twenty-six bodies that have shown up around the five boroughs, considering most of them died just about the same way as Pac Man. But like I said, bikers are like that.

Back on February 3rd or 4th, I came close to telling Harry what had happened to me. We took a ride down to the Jersey shore on an unusually warm winter day and had a few beers, but I just couldn't tell him.

He still asks me what happened to Caroline. I *still* tell him I don't know, or that she must've taken off for some mysterious reason. Maybe one day I'll tell him how I came home last week to find her in bed with one of the idiots who'd streaked with us that night. I kicked his ass good, then sat on *her* chest, asking why she would disrespect me in our own bed.

She spat in my face.

I hated to ruin such a nice pair, but it did feel nice, the blade slamming down between her soft breasts. Tough chick: she didn't even scream.

The cops haven't found her yet, which is surprising, considering I put her body in a dumpster behind a Dunkin' Donuts in Queens. There are either no homeless people in that area, or the trash pick-up is real lousy.

I'll probably tell Harry all of this one day. I'll probably tell him I'm the infamous *Moon Killer*, a name provided by the media—all of my victims' deaths have been determined to occur around midnight.

They should know how ironic that name is.

But for now, I'm heading out west to a biker rally in California. Maybe I'll stay there a while. Maybe I'll grab a job at some garage and see if Californians treat their rides as poorly as New Yorkers do. Or maybe I'll just hang there a bit for a change of scenery.

Bikers are like that.

WHISKER WHIPPED

Author's Note: This one was for a benefit anthology titled 'HAMSTERS!' It was a blast to write, and as an animal lover I simply had to add another creature into the mix.

He wasn't sure if it was the niacin tablets he'd read about on some men's health website, or his recent departure from fried foods. Perhaps it was the twenty-minute daily exercise routine he began seven weeks ago, or maybe a combination of the three lifestyle changes. Whatever he'd done, it was working. And as Lisa pushed him down on his back and impaled herself, Frank looked at the clock and couldn't believe they'd been at it for close to an hour…and he had yet to climax. Gripping her ass cheeks, he pulled her down onto himself with the vigor of a twenty-year-old, not a man approaching fifty. Another half-hour went by before he knew it, and they changed positions. Doggy style, then back to missionary with Lisa's legs pinned behind her head Bugs-Bunny style, then back to her on top.

A few times during their session, Frank worried he would have a heart attack or, at the least, blow his back out, but nothing happened. And less than a minute after they both came, Frank was ready to go again.

But that would have to wait. Lisa had jumped out of bed and dressed in record time when Squeaky nonchalantly crawled out from between Frank's legs and made his way up to rest on her pillow. As she cursed and questioned what the hell was wrong with him, Frank and Squeaky lay still and silent and watched her stomp out the door. Frank knew they'd never see her again.

Frank put Squeaky back in his tank, then booted up his laptop. He'd find someone else. There was *always* someone else.

***

A two-week dry spell put Frank on edge. No one had answered his ad on four different hook-up sites (*Straight white male in great shape looking for adventurous NSA relationship in NYC area. Your pic gets mine*), and a slight depression moved in. He came close to stopping by Burger King on the way home from work one day, but managed to keep driving. When he arrived home, he went through his workout routine for the second time that day, and then had some grilled tilapia with steamed asparagus. He popped his daily niacin tablet and a host of assorted vitamins, mostly Bs, as dessert.

Frank plopped down on the couch, exhausted, but decided to check for messages before turning on the tube. He jumped back up and booted the laptop. He snacked on a banana as the computer came to life. Within two minutes, he was online.

He smiled as he noticed that two messages had come in from two of the sites. The first reply sounded iffy and there was no picture attached, which was always a bad sign. *Delete.* The second reply sounded much more promising, *and* there was an attachment. Frank decided to read the note first before seeing what the writer looked like.

Hey, Frank B. This is Chloe R. I'm adventurous and looking for a steady NSA situation in NYC myself. If you like my pic, please send me yours. Hoping to hear from you soon.

Frank started downloading the moment he finished reading. Within seconds, Chloe R.'s picture filled his computer screen. She wasn't overweight and wasn't a rail. She had a build like *Xena*. He'd always had a thing for the Warrior Princess, and while Chloe didn't look like her, she had the same figure, and to Frank's surprise, was even better looking. And she claimed to be adventurous. He tapped the reply tab and hoped this was for real. Lisa had claimed to be adventurous, too, but had freaked out as soon as she saw Squeaky.

Frank attached a full-body shot of himself on the beach while vacationing in Florida, wrote a short note (*You're very pretty and I hope you find me attractive too*), then hit send.

Chloe replied again ten minutes later. It contained her cell phone number and an urgent message to call her as soon as possible, even now, if he was around.

Frank and Chloe spoke for fifteen minutes. They made plans to meet at his place tomorrow night at eight o'clock. She laughed when he asked if she'd like to meet for dinner somewhere, and unlike Lisa and the countless women before her, she reminded him that they'd met on a sex hookup website, so why waste time with the typical dating bullshit?

They spoke for another half hour before she said she needed to get some sleep, especially since she didn't plan on getting much the next night.

Excited and contemplating calling in sick the next morning, Frank lay in bed with Squeaky on his chest. He petted the Tibetan dwarf hamster he'd special ordered almost a year ago, wondering how some people could consider these beautiful creatures pests.

"We're going to have a good time tomorrow, my friend," Frank said, running his index finger down the rodent's short back. "This one sounds much more teachable than Lisa. Remember the last one, who ran out of here the second she saw you?"

Squeaky looked at Frank as if he understood what he was saying.

"Adventurous, my ass!" Frank stood up and placed his pet back in its cage. "We'll see if Chloe understands the meaning of the word. So far *no one* has."

Frank fell asleep less than five minutes after he shut off the lights, hoping tomorrow would be the start of something special.

* * *

Frank figured that staying home would cause time to stand still, so he went to work and had a decent day. His boss was on a business trip, so things had been mellow around the office lately. Yeah, Frank thought, good thing not to waste a sick day while the douchebag was away.

He arrived home by 4:30, had some grilled chicken and a mixed vegetable side, worked out, took his niacin and other vitamins, and by a little after 6 decided to spend the next two hours online while he waited for Chloe.

He checked the other sites out of curiosity, but saw no replies to his ads. It didn't bother him. If Chloe turned out to be even half as amazing as she sounded, he wouldn't have to worry about checking ads for a long time.

Two quick rings took his mind off the men's health site he was surfing. He shut the laptop and said into the intercom, "Chloe?"

"That's me."

Frank hit the buzzer and let her into the building. Less than two minutes later there was a knock on the door.

Chloe was at least four inches taller than him, and even prettier in person. She wore a long beige trench coat, and for a second Frank worried she was going to pull out two Uzis and start shooting. But his apprehension faded when she unbuttoned the coat. She wasn't wearing anything underneath.

"Is this okay?" she said as she placed her lone garment on a kitchen chair.

"That's fine," he said, feeling incredibly awkward as he stared at this beautiful woman wearing nothing but a pair of low-cut pink Puma sneakers. It looked like Chloe wasn't kidding when she said she was adventurous, and he hoped he had enough condoms in his nightstand. Any woman who showed up at a stranger's house naked had to be a bit insane, and Frank had the feeling that things were about to get wild.

Before he finished his thought, she pulled him close, her breasts squishing against his chest. "If you don't mind me saying so, you look *so* much better in person."

"I just said the same thing to myself about you."

Chloe wrapped her hands around his head and began kissing him. Frank dove right in, kissing back and undressing at the same time.

"You like that?" she asked, pulling back from him.

"You're quite the kisser."

Chloe dropped to her knees and took Frank in her mouth. He leaned back against the sink and wondered how long it had been since she got laid. She went at him as if her life depended on it, taking his entire length like it was nothing, making sounds that almost brought him to the end. Just when he thought he was going to burst, she stood up and led him by his cock to the bedroom, as if she'd been here before. At first this bothered him, but he figured, how different could one apartment be from the next?

She lay on the bed and pushed his head down between her legs. He lapped at her with vigor, despite her long legs nearly crushing his neck a few times. He got off on the loud groans she made as he went to town. After what must've been fifteen minutes, he stood up and opened the nightstand.

He ripped the condom wrapper open with his teeth and began to unroll it over his raging erection.

"Umm, what are you doing?"

"What does it look like I'm doing?" he asked, confused.

Chloe stood up next to him and pulled the rubber off. "What was all that shit about you looking for someone *adventurous*? What kind of adventure is this?"

Frank stood back for a moment, then said, "Listen, *you* don't want anything and *I* don't want anything, right?"

"Well, *I don't* have anything. Do you?"

"I'm clean as a whistle."

"Then what's the problem?"

Frank looked at Chloe and let her words sink in. While his idea of adventure wasn't fucking someone he'd just met without protection, he'd read that a lot of people who met on these sites took risks like this. Apparently Chloe was one of them.

"Frank? You still here?"

"Yeah. Sorry. It's just…I—"

"Listen. We just went down on each other. If I had something, and if you had something, we'd both have caught it already, right?"

Frank wasn't sure how true that was, but it made sense.

He climbed on top of her without any further hesitation, and they kissed until his erection fully returned.

He hammered into her for close to half an hour, her legs wrapped around his back, pushing him in with every thrust. Frank then flipped her into doggy style, then sideways, then back to missionary. When he couldn't hold back any longer, which was over an hour later, he pulled out and released himself all over her stomach and tits. She smiled and turned onto her side, as if she wasn't a sticky mess.

"Be right back," Frank said. On the way out of his room, he grabbed Squeaky out of the cage. He peed, then washed his hands. Squeaky watched from the side of the sink.

"Okay, buddy. Let's do this."

He picked up his beloved pet and headed back to the bedroom.

* * *

Chloe turned out to be as adventurous a woman as Frank had ever seen or even read about. The moment he returned from the bathroom, he surprised her by going right back at it, as if they hadn't just spent over an hour in full-throttle action. As he banged her up against the bedroom wall, she had asked "Viagra?" to which Frank replied, "Never touch that shit."

Chloe even did something *no one* had ever done. She got down on all fours and offered him her ass. Frank thought, *Well, if she* does *have anything, I'm about to get it.*

It wasn't as easy as the porn stars made it look. While Frank wasn't huge—he had a respectable, thick seven inches, and had a hard time getting even a quarter of it inside. After only a few minutes, he stopped and put it back inside her pussy, continuing to hit her from behind. He couldn't tell if she was pissed off about his lack of anal skills, but eventually she began groaning again, especially when he laid down on the cool wood floor and pulled her on top of him.

She slid down his shaft and looked at him as if they were doing it for the first time. Frank felt harder than ever, especially with Squeaky leaning against his prostate. The critter's whiskers massaged his insides, heightening every sensation. He felt as if his cock would reach her heart and stop it, killing her in a bout of passion like no other.

Chloe moaned louder than ever. "Don't stop...you're right there!" She continued sliding up and down, faster than before, and it was during this brief time that Frank realized she hadn't come during their first session.

He looked down and saw himself sliding in and out. He felt her grip on his shoulders tighten and knew she was ready to explode.

And explode she did.

Chloe lifted herself off Frank as orgasm hit. While Frank let his seed fly, she squirted like a dam that had just burst, soaking Frank, the side of the bed, and the floor. And when they finished wetting each other, Chloe lay atop him, kissing his face all over in appreciation. Apparently her little issue had freaked other men out, but not Frank. He found it to be quite a turn-on.

Chloe finally rolled onto her back next to Frank, and Frank did his little wiggle that let Squeaky know it was time to come out.

The Tibetan dwarf pulled itself up over Frank's spent nut sac into Chloe's waiting view. But instead of screaming and running from the house, she petted it and said, "Oh my God! How cute! What's his name?"

"Squeaky," Frank said. He put his arm around Chloe. She nestled herself as she took the hamster into her hand and kissed it on the nose.

"A tough-looking guy like you naming your pet Squeaky? That's just adorable."

"Adorable?"

Chloe laughed, and then placed Squeaky on his chest.

"I'd like for you to meet someone, too."

At first, Frank thought she was going to show him a picture on her cell phone. But as she spread her legs, he remembered her jacket was in the kitchen, and who knew if she'd even brought a phone with her?

"Frank," Chloe said, squinting. "I want you to…meet…"

Frank slid away from her to allow room for whatever she was about to reveal.

Something slowly made its way out of Chloe's ass. She screamed so loud Frank had to put his hand over her mouth. The last thing he needed was the old bag upstairs reporting him again.

This wasn't a hamster, gerbil, or mouse. Whatever it was had a small head, which was followed by a lengthy neck that slid out of her, taking its sweet time. By the time the thing had come out, it stood at least five feet tall, and looked down at Frank as if in disapproval.

Chloe said, "This is Gordy. Say hi!"

Frank looked on in disbelief as the beast skidded around, trying to find purchase in the love puddle they'd made all over the wood floor.

"H-hi," Frank said.

Chloe laughed. "Oh, don't be so surprised! Tell me he's not cute!"

Something inside Frank snapped. He took Squeaky and ran into the bathroom, locking the door. When she realized he wasn't coming back out, Chloe began cursing him, calling him a hypocrite and every name under the sun. It seemed like hours before she finally stopped yelling, and he heard the door slam.

He patted Squeaky in relief, tickling its whiskers that he loved so much, apologizing to it and thanking every God he could think of that Chloe's monster didn't eat his beloved pet.

* * *

It took Frank two hours to clean his apartment. He didn't realize what a huge mess they'd made, but the worst of it wasn't from him or Chloe. He never knew baby giraffes could shit so much, and then he became a bit happier, realizing his lack of anal skills wasn't his fault.

ANTIBACTERIAL POPE

Author's Note: One of the first bizarro pieces I had published, and still a favorite of many of my readers. I had Rod Kierkegaard's "Rock Opera" in mind as I wrote this. Rock Opera was one of the weirdest things ever created, a comic strip featured in (the illustrated) Heavy Metal Magazine back in the 1980s.

"They're at it again," the Pope said as he poured fresh cement into the bullet hole.

The audience continued chant-renditions of forgotten television jingles, clouds becoming triangular in the east.

"But Father, can we truly afford to lose the people? Father, can we..." A circle appeared under Cardinal O'Henry and sucked him down.

See the planes: unfueled, yet they fly.

O'Henry, released on a frozen tundra, founds his own sect.

"I just want you to know how much this means to me," an audience member said, his exposed arms covered in clear gelatin.

"Don't speak, my child."

Police rushed the altar. The pistol floated before the crowd, daring them to look at it. One policeman dared and was rewarded with two holes above his right eye.

O'Henry: "We have to get some heat or we'll die—and it'll be hard to attract any new members."

See the planes: tiny excremental meteors falling from their wings.

"Forgive me, Father; it's been six years since my last panic attack."

The Pope closed his eyes and poured hardening cement into the confessor's ears. A circle formed beneath the now-deaf man.

Hear the planes, those of aural cohesiveness.

Antennae sprouted from the policeman's wounds and fired two shots at the cement-crazed pontiff.

O'Henry: "Brothers and sisters, truly we are cursed. No one remembers a word I've said. You...yes, you who just joined us. What do you have to say for yourself?"

The now deaf man shrugged his shoulders, said "What?" then succumbed to another mental blow.

See the planes: crashing into the square, one by one by one, unfueled yet exploding.

Covered in cement, the Pope escaped and headed for the tundra.

O'Henry sensed the pontiff's coming, still screaming as ice worms pulled his extracted brain across the solid-white plain.

See the planes: debris.

See the pontiff: frost-bit and sluggish.

See the crowd: a circle forming underneath them.

O'Henry: fallen, now promoted.

THE SATANIC RITES OF SASQUATCH

Author's Note: Bigfoot and Yeti stories/films exploded in the 2000s, so I figured why not blend both legendary creatures with a healthy dose of Satanism? And yes, the title is an ode to the similar-sounding Christopher Lee film.

Somewhere in the Pacific Northwest, the creature remained silent, unmoving. Its keen sense of hearing zeroed in on the two figures sitting before a small fire.

* * *

"I'm telling you," one of them said as he removed his gloves to rub his hands over the flame, "there really hasn't been a significant sighting since Mount Saint Helens blew her lid back in—what was it—eighty-three?"

His partner continued chewing a sandwich as he replied, "Eighty. I'm not arguing with that. What I'd like to prove is that they still exist. You can't tell me that in all these years, Mount Saint Helens was the first disaster they had to deal with?"

"Of course not. But I'm betting even *they* don't speak to each other with their mouths full."

"Bite me, mom."

A rustling in the trees interrupted the USC archeology students.

"Did you—"

"Shhh. Yes, I heard it."

One man led with a rifle, his partner trailing with a compact digital camcorder. When they came through the circle of trees surrounding their campsite, they noticed a set of large footprints in the snow.

"Look!" Timothy kneeled next to the closest one. "We've only been here two days and already we're finding tracks. Is the camera on?"

"Of course—go ahead."

"This is Timothy Hanley, coming to you from Skamania County, Washington. On our second day of expedition, we've just come across these unusual footprints that seem too big to be human—unless the Lakers have a game close by—and a bit too human-shaped to be from any animal known to man."

John Johnstone raised the camera.

"What are you doing?"

"Just keep talking...I'm following the tracks before the snow covers them."

Timothy continued. "I'm taking measurements now... this print is almost three inches deep, and...WOW!...twenty-eight inches in length! I believe the longest recorded was twenty-four—"

"Tim! Look!"

Timothy stood up but couldn't see anything but descending footprints and lightly falling snow.

"Here, I have it on zoom," John said as he handed over the cam.

Timothy stuck his eye in the viewfinder. His jaw dropped. "Let's move!" He tucked the rifle under his arm and took off after the tall, dark figure. It ran over a slight incline and out of view.

* * *

The creature decided to take a chance. It made its way to the campfire and sniffed around. It ripped open a duffel bag loaded with assorted snacks and began to feast, wrappers and all. Another bag was full of water bottles, which it consumed within seconds.

"It's going that way!"

The creature heard the man speak and stopped chewing, water flowing down its hairy chin. The voice came from one of the men it had been eavesdropping on.

When the creature had come into their campsite clearing, it'd watched the two men running away. It picked a piece of plastic from its back teeth.

The creature began following them when it looked down and noticed three sets of tracks. One set was too big to be from either of the small fire-makers. Upon closer inspection, it realized the print was almost the same size as its own.

Trouble.

Had its mate or another member of its family left the cave without permission? Had one of the young decided it was now old enough to go off on its own?

The usually easygoing creature's brownish complexion turned red as it unleashed a murderous howl.

* * *

Timothy and John stopped dead in their tracks.

"P-please tell me that was a coyote?"

John turned around, looking through the cam, and saw nothing but snowfall and their human footprints. "It sure sounded like one—"

"*Sure sounded like one*? We've been here two days and haven't seen or heard anything besides birds and squirrels! How would you even know what a coyote sounds like?"

"I have no idea what one sounds like. Why did you ask?" John said as he turned back around. "Let's just keep after—"

"Crap! He's gone!"

John zoomed ahead toward an open plain. The tracks they'd been chasing went to the middle of the field, then vanished—at least as far as he could see.

"See anything?"

"Nope."

"CRAP!"

With less than an hour before nightfall, the amateur archeologists decided to return to camp with the hopes of picking up again come morning.

* * *

"See! I told you it was a coyote!"

Ripped duffel bags and emptied food containers littered the camp area.

"I doubt a coyote did this," John said. He pointed to tracks that looked similar to those they'd been following, although these tracks were deeper and longer and hard to follow.

Timothy snapped pictures of the frantic footprint pattern.

Another hair-raising howl came from deep in the forest. Timothy cocked his rifle out of instinct.

"Will you relax? You're the one who's always said these things aren't violent toward humans."

"I-I know. But this is the first time I've heard—wait a minute—so you're saying you think this is a Sasquatch? *A Bigfoot*?"

"I'm saying these aren't like any tracks or howls I've ever seen or heard."

Timothy smiled, then went back on guard.

"Plus, I don't think a coyote or even a bear could've eaten all the food we had." John picked up two large bags of ranch Doritos, ten crushed (and emptied) cans of Spam and two empty cases of Slim Jims. He almost cried when he noticed the tattered shopping bag that had been full of hero sandwiches. The two dozen eggs they'd brought were gone, too.

Yet another howl rang out. Its force seemed to tilt the treetops.

"It came from that way!" John said, clicking his cam back on. "Let's go!"

Timothy wasn't crazy about the approaching darkness, but figured the snow would give them enough light to find their way back. He took the lead with his rifle aimed straight ahead. He noticed tracks coming in and out of their campsite. "Whatever ruined our camp must've been waiting for us to leave."

"Nice observation, Einstein."

Timothy grinned and tried to decide if he was more excited about proving the existence of a legendary creature or putting two holes in the head of whatever ate their food.

* * *

"What the—"

"Shhhh! Zip your pie-hole, will you?" John said as they ducked behind a three-foot tall rock.

"Okay. Just don't mention food again."

A tremendous snow-covered mountain seemed to give off its own light. At its base was the entrance to what John assumed was a large cave. But what really took his breath away was the scene playing out as night swallowed the landscape.

A stark-naked man was tied to a table-sized slab of stone, his nipples hard as bullets in the frigid January air; he whimpered for help as if he'd been there for hours. His feet and hands were visibly red, even from this distance.

"We've got to help him."

"PLEASE shut up!" John said. "Of course we will. Let's just make sure whoever did this is gone."

Timothy pointed ahead with a worried look.

Several figures came from the cave entrance. John figured they each had to be at least seven feet tall. Their faces and bodies were covered with dark robes. They surrounded their captive, six on each side.

John wiped sweat from his eyes but continued filming.

After the figures placed their arms on the sides of the stone table, a 13th figure came forth, its robe a dark shade of red and decorated with ancient-looking symbols.

John zoomed in tight. The arms of each figure were covered in dark hair, their fingers ape-like. He offered the cam to Timothy, who took a peek before handing it back. Timothy crossed himself…a weird thing to do, given he was an atheist.

Then the figure in red lowered its hood.

"For the love of Moses," John said, a surprising comment from another admitted atheist.

The man on the stone table stopped squirming, looking up at the ape-like beast as it revealed itself from its unusual garb.

"You. Human." The creature leaned down and picked up a pair of custom boots made to leave prints that mocked its own. "We haven't seen this kind of foolishness in many moons. Why does your kind insist on trying to expose us?"

Timothy grabbed John's arm. "T-they *talk*?"

"Apparently," John said, as if this revelation wasn't too much of a surprise.

The creatures around the altar began chanting in all-too-human tones.

"I wasn't trying to expose you!" the captive said, tears forming in his eyes. "I was just trying to mess with my friends—they're the ones up here trying to expose you!"

John zoomed into the captive's face.

"Who is it?" Timothy asked as he made two fists.

"Professor Hinderman!"

"That son of a—"

"I told you he thought we were crazy for taking this trip."

Timothy stood up, but John pulled him right back down. "Cool it! Just sit tight."

The Sasquatch coven leader continued. "That's a good one, human. We've heard that one about a thousand times." Then the creature lifted his hands. "Disrobe!"

The coven dropped their garments in unison. Twelve Bigfoots stood at attention. The one closest to the leader handed him a snake-shaped dagger.

"N-no! It was just a prank! HELP! I swear...I'll get rid of the boots!"

"Great SasKarSasKar, hear us. Great SasKarSasKar, please accept this offering in return for your protection."

John forced himself to look as the blade came down into his archeology professor's chest. He noticed Timothy squinting from the corner of his eye.

The head Sasquatch ripped Hinderman's heart out, took a bite, then passed it around the table. Each member took a bite, then kneeled after doing so.

"Great SasKarSasKar, we praise you for your—"

A swarm of white-haired creatures popped out of nowhere and dragged the leader down. Claws flew and blood spurted. The leader cried out in agony. "Run, my children! Run!"

The Bigfoots scattered in twelve different directions. One of them came toward John and Timothy. It ran past them, stopped and looked back. "More humans?"

They sat speechless. *Petrified.*

"No time for this. Follow me!" it said.

They followed the creature without hesitation. John asked, "What are those things?"

"I'll tell you when—if—we get away."

John kept only a few paces behind the Sasquatch. Timothy fell further behind with each step.

"Come on, man! Move it!" John said.

"I-I can't. I'm not gonna—"

Two white-haired creatures took Timothy down.

Fear kept John's blood pumping, his legs moving at a pace he never would've believed possible. The sound of his friend's screams gave him another burst of speed.

A smaller mountain appeared in a clearing. John followed the Sasquatch into a cramped opening near its base and collapsed from exhaustion.

"You can't stop now." The beast threw John over its shoulder like a rag doll. It continued inward, John shielding his head with his right arm from occasional slams into the ceiling.

When they reached a primitive-looking chamber, the beast slid a tremendous boulder across the entranceway and braced it with several logs.

As John opened his mouth, the beast said, "Shhh. Catch your breath. We're going to be here a while."

Along the walls, John noticed canteens and other various kinds of camping equipment hanging from vines and makeshift shelves. The beast took a sip from one canteen, then handed it to him. "Drink."

John took a sip. As he swallowed, the madness of his predicament overtook him.

He passed out.

* * *

"I said wake up!"

Thinking he was in his dorm room, John rolled over and threw his arm around Theresa. Although his girlfriend was Italian, he didn't remember her being this hairy. He opened his eyes and realized he was lying next to the creature that had saved his life. His pulse rose.

"I didn't know if you'd wake," the creature said as it sat up. Even sitting, it was taller than John when he stood.

"What were those things? Why did they attack you? Why did you kill my professor?"

"Ah! So you did know the other human!" The Sasquatch rubbed its chin. "But that's all in the past. I went back to our temple as you slept. As far as I can tell, they killed my entire family. And it looks like most of *them* have been destroyed, too."

"W-who did? W-who are *them*?"

"Those damn Yetis. One of you stupid humans brought a couple here from Tibet many moons ago. They multiplied quickly. We've been at war ever since. At least this time I found many of them dead, too."

John's mind reeled. Sasquatch. Yeti. Creatures he'd mocked Timothy for believing in had turned out to be all too real. He wiped sweat from his forehead. "Where are they now?"

"The Yetis live high up on our temple's mountain. They only descend when we perform our sacrifices, which we don't do too often. But it's something we've been doing for centuries, and it's a chance we must take regardless. The Great SasKarSasKar has been protecting us since the dawn of time, and keeps our existence secret from humans. If not for the Yetis, we'd always live in peace."

The creature's deep voice fascinated John more than its massive size. "Are there others of your kind?"

"Unless one of our coven escaped and is in hiding, I'm the last." The creature lay back down. "And I need you to help me. It's long past due for my kind to take the offensive."

"How can I help you with that?"

The creature held its massive index finger to John's mouth. "Shhhh.

It's going to take some time. Patience, my dear." It ripped off John's jacket and rubbed his chest. "Just follow my lead."

John tried to pull away. The Sasquatch bared its teeth. *Her* teeth.

"O-okay!" John said. "Okay! What do you want me to do?"

The creature pulled the rest of John's clothes off and sat above him. "I want you to do *me*."

John squirmed as the monster rubbed itself over his crotch. Its smell repulsed him. He begged it to stop.

"Do what you have to do to get it up. You will help my kind to survive...or you will be my dinner."

With no other choice, John forced himself to relax. The creature continued rubbing itself over his groin. He tried to picture the first time he'd been intimate with Theresa. He tried with everything he had to force the creature's smell out of his system.

Eventually, he became ready.

"That's it. Good human."

John and the Sasquatch eventually made a connection. John forced a look through cracked eyelids. Was the creature smirking due to his non-Sasquatch size? Would he even be able to impregnate another species? And what was the story with the pentagrams and inverted crosses painted all over the cave's walls?

"Oh, yes! That's it!" The Sasquatch rode John faster and faster. He was surprised by how well his imagination helped him do what needed to be done to stay alive.

"You like that?" John said, trying to keep his mind sane.

"Me like! Me like!"

John managed to turn the beast on her back. He thrust into her as her vice-like legs wrapped around him. It felt like he was in the grip of a giant tarantula.

"Me like! Me like!"

"Who's your daddy?"

"You my daddy! You my daddy!"

John climaxed and immediately passed out, questioning his sanity.

***

Timothy woke up freezing. He was wrapped in several blankets, but icy wind blew in through a nearby opening. As he gained consciousness, he realized he was in a cave. He squirmed over to the opening and almost puked when he looked down. The cave was high up on a mountain. His fear of heights kicked into overdrive. He remembered who must've brought him here.

"It's about time you woke."

Timothy turned around to see a white-haired creature squatting right next to him. He blacked out.

A few seconds later, the thing had woken him back up by splashing snow into his face. "Stop doing that! I need your cooperation," it said as it began undressing him, licking its lips.

Timothy screamed and tried to blink himself away…but the snow and wind kept him alert.

THE AIRCRASH BUREAU

(Or, How Johnny Carson and General Patton Hijacked a Space Shuttle to Get Back on the Air)

Author's Note: I think out of all the stories I've written, I had the most fun with this one. It incorporates some TV as well as real-life characters I've always been fond of. And I think this shows you can be as strange as you want and still keep a coherent, if somewhat dream-like story.

"It's the *Tomorrow Night Show*, with your host, Johnny Carson. Tonight's guests are Yankee legend Mickey Mantle ... from TV's *The Honeymooners*, actor and comedian Jackie Gleason ... and your musical guest, the lovely and talented Janis Joplin. And now, heeeeeeeere's Johnnn-y—"

Ed McMahon's head exploded like a rotted cantaloupe dropped from a skyscraper. When the stage cleared of smoke, the gunman took a seat on the famed couch.

"I think we've all had enough of him," the gunman said as he removed his helmet and lit a cigar.

"General George S. Patton, ladies and gentlemen," Johnny Carson said with a warm smile. "Let's all give him a big hand!"

General Patton stood, saluted the cheering audience, and walked back over to the former co-host's body. He picked it up and carried it to the left edge of the stage. As if flicking his stogie ash, he dumped the headless corpse into the black abyss. The crowd went wild in appreciation.

After the General (and new co-host) was re-seated, Johnny said, "So, General George Patton; what have you been up to?"

"I'll tell you, Johnny," he said while shifting the cigar across his lip, "things kind of slowed down since the war ended. I received a call a few weeks ago, asking me to work for that kid who comes on after you, but I couldn't handle staying up that late every night."

"Even though we *don't* really sleep around here?"

Patton turned and stared Johnny down. "You being smart with me or something?"

Johnny held his hands up in mock surrender. "Would I do that to a four-star general?"

Patton and Johnny tilted their heads back and laughed. They both slapped the *Tomorrow Night Show*'s desk. Carson's cup tipped over. Liquid splashed his tie, which caused the hosts to laugh harder. A holographic image of Dom DeLuise's face appeared between the two men until they regained control.

Patton fired a shot. The bullet picked off a man who stood in the back row. It sent him over the railing. His falling scream caused the audience to cheer and encourage the hosts to continue.

"Okay, folks—okay," Johnny said. "If you want to keep wooing, the Apollo's right on the next plane!"

Along with the crowd, Patton's laughs returned, delaying the first guest's air time. Eventually, things settled. Johnny adjusted his soiled tie.

"Our first guest tonight was the star of one of the most beloved television programs in history. Although he went on to star in countless films, he'll always be best known as Brooklyn's greatest bus driver. Won't you please welcome Mr. Jackie Gleason."

Dressed in his *Honeymooners* bus driver's outfit, Gleason glided across the stage, his arms waving as he did his famous dance.

The crowd began chanting, "Television. Television. Television."

Gleason bowed to the audience, then turned and shook Johnny's hand. Patton stood and saluted. Gleason returned the gesture, then everyone took their seats.

"So, Jackie Gleason. How long has it been?"

The audience continued chanting, "Television, television, television," their voices now whispered.

"Quite a while, my friend." Gleason looked around the studio. "Nice joint you got here."

A lone voice chuckled toward the rear of the studio audience.

"Did I say something funny?" Out of instinct, Gleason ducked when a BOOM! sounded next to his head. General Patton tucked his pistol back into its holder as the lone giggler's screams descended into the abyss.

* * *

GENERAL GEORGE S. PATTON: MISSION SEMI-ACCOMPLISHED ON THE *TOMORROW NIGHT SHOW.* TRANSFER BACK TO SICILY CURRENTLY IN PROGRESS.

* * *

General Patton held his helmet with both hands. He felt like a chunk of prematurely chewed meat being sucked through an infant's esophagus by a hydraulic vacuum.

* * *

SICILY. 1943.

The United States' Seventh Army Division cruised alongside the British Eighth Army just west of Palermo. According to intelligence, most of the German troops had headed east toward Messina, but those left behind fell swiftly under Allied gunfire and bayonet strike.

Patton stood atop his tank, looking down as his men piled up a couple dozen bodies.

"Fantastic job, gentlemen. Now let's do this fine city proud."

Eight Italian-American Marines kneeled around the pile of enemy corpses. Each of their mouths opened wider than seemed humanly possible. Strands of shredded cheese flew out from each soldier's midsection, evenly covering the pile of death. When they finished, Patton motioned for two soldiers with flamethrowers to come forth.

"Okay, boys...bake these bastards!"

The intense heat quickly melted the mixed Italian cheeses onto dead German flesh. The scent gave General Patton a partial erection, but his focus remained straight.

"Okay, gentlemen, we move east."

***

"Permission to speak," General Patton said.

PERMISSION GRANTED.

"I need to get back to the *Tomorrow Night Show*."

IT'S NOT TIME. WE NEED YOU TO HEAD THE TROOPS EAST TOWARD...

"I know what my orders are. But there are also more bastards in that audience who need to be dealt with."

DO YOU THINK WE DON'T KNOW WHAT WE'RE DOING, GENERAL?

"Sometimes I wonder—"

* * *

GENERAL GEORGE S. PATTON ONCE AGAIN INSUBORDINATE. NEW ASSIGNNMENT: UNITED STATES OF AMERICA. KENNEDY SPACE CENTER, FLORIDA. 1981. PROTECT LAUNCH OF SPACE SHUTTLE *COLUMBIA* FROM CROCAGATOR ASSAULT.

* * *

At first, the General thought the scream was in reaction to his nakedness. But when he cleared his eyes of swamp water, he realized it was coming from a young girl, whose attention had drifted from the shuttle launch and over to him as he wrestled the fifteen-foot crocagator.

"Shhhhh," he said to the blonde-haired kid, easily no more than ten years old. "Don't mind me, darlin' ... you're gonna miss the launch."

The ship's massive engines fired up, bringing the girl's attention back where it belonged. General Patton took the opportunity to pull the two-headed beast—the last of fifteen—back under the muck. The thing's tail clanged off his head: for some reason his superiors had left him with his helmet, and something had been bopping around underneath it since his assault began.

A monstrous flash let him know the shuttle had launched. Knowing everyone's eyes would be on the modern marvel, he came up for air. The crocagator seemed to become more powerful as time passed. This time it snapped the spear that had slain its comrades.

"Maybe this'll get you outta my hair," General Patton said as he head-butted the croc in the gator-face section. The beast seemed momentarily stunned. When he adjusted his helmet, he finally realized what had been sliding around atop his scalp the past few hours. In a motion quicker than the slickest sheriff from an Old Western, Patton grabbed his trusty pistol and pulled off four shots—each one hitting the crocagator's four eyeballs. The beast wore a toothy smirk of defeat as it sank to its grave.

Just as he caught his breath, General Patton felt a hand on his shoulder. He spun around with his dripping pistol still drawn.

"Hey—it's me!"

"Johnny?"

"In the flesh."

"How in God's name did you get here?"

"Let's just say Gleason owed me a favor."

General Patton smiled. "At least someone cares what's going on with the show."

"Tell me about it. Don't your Superiors realize Alexander and Montgomery pretty much have things under control over in Messina?"

"I guess not. Hey, how did you get here?"

Johnny held up a fist full of gray matter.

"Is that—?"

"Yes. Now, when's that thing supposed to come back down?"

Patton looked up, as if he could see how high the shuttle had climbed. "No idea, my friend."

"Then I guess we'll have to wait—"

"WAIT my ass!" General Patton said, pointing to a humongous hangar not far from the site of the launch.

* * *

CARSON HAS ENOUGH MCBRAIN TO GET BACK.

A seldom-vocal second Superior said, SON OF A BITCH.

* * *

Under the cover of darkness, General George S. Patton and Johnny

Carson approached the poorly lit hangar. Carson's suit was saturated, while Patton's tight-fitting NASA jump suit would work for now; he hated to knock out such a fine young man, but those were the risks you took when you had the farthest look-out point at the facility—not to mention, space travel would probably be much too uncomfortable in nothing but a helmet.

"WOW! Aren't you—?"

"Johnny Carson!" Johnny Carson said as he cracked the seasoned officer in the chin with a frozen turkey.

"Where on God's green earth did you pull that out from?" Patton asked, his cast-iron lips lonely without a cigar.

"You'd be surprised what I've accumulated after hosting this show for so long."

The bird quickly dried out and jigged into a patch of shrubs.

"WOW—aren't you—?"

"General George S. Patton!!" General George S. Patton said as he knocked the next officer's teeth out of his head with a right hook. "United States Army!"

Johnny dragged the body out of their way. Within five minutes, the talk show hosts had fifteen unconscious guards on their hands.

"Let's do this." General Patton led the way down a narrow corridor toward a second shuttle.

Johnny whistled when they stood under the shuttle. General Patton removed his helmet to admire the fine piece of engineering.

A deafening alarm rang out.

Johnny followed the General underneath the ship. "Any idea how we get in?" he asked.

"The only way I know." The General and Johnny booked up a service ladder. "You sure you have enough stuff?"

"Plenty."

Patton fired at the side window. The first shot barely cracked the glass. The second weakened it. Then Johnny forced his right shoe into the crack. "Take cover!"

Both men ducked with their fingers in their ears. The shoe blew the window out without damaging the shuttle's sides.

"I like your toys, soldier," General Patton said as Johnny jumped in first.

Screams of "Stop!" and "Halt!" echoed throughout the hangar as soon as they stood up. Johnny rubbed a bit of Ed McMahon's brain matter around the perimeter of the broken window. A flesh-like barrier instantly sealed it. "Now let's get outta here," he said, knowing the General wasn't one to follow orders.

"Watch it there, buddy-boy, or I'll have you doing push-ups on the roof of this thing once we get out of the earth's gravitational pull."

"Gotcha."

It took nearly half an hour for the talk show hosts to figure out how to start Space Shuttle *Columbia 2*, and if not for Patton's excellent tank training, their escape would have ended here; the controls were remarkably similar.

The shuttle crashed through the hangar's closed doors, then headed down the runway.

"But how do you plan to get us—"

"Just relax, soldier."

Patton smiled as the reanimated crocagators swarmed the facility and overtook everyone who attempted to chase the shuttle. "Beautiful...kill 'em all! Eat 'em all alive!"

Johnny thumbed through a loose-leaf binder he'd grabbed on the way into the cockpit. "I'll be right back."

When he returned a few minutes later, Patton said, "Where did you go?"

"I found the interior fuel-additive valve. Ed's about to do his thing."

Without the aid of lift-off engines or additional thrusters, the Space Shuttle *Columbia 2* took off for the heavens like a pigeon being chased by a hawk. Johnny smeared some McBrain up and around the General's nostrils and mouth, and then did the same to himself.

Within minutes they were out of the earth's pull. Mere seconds after that, the combination of American-made shuttle fuel and Ed McMahon's brain matter took both men into the plane of the *Tomorrow Night Show*.

* * *

Johnny Carson crashed through his famous desk as General Patton slammed through the plush guest-couch.

"All right, folks, we're back," Johnny said as he helped the General out of the cushions. The drop from the shuttle to the *Tomorrow Night Show*'s set disintegrated both men's clothing, although Patton's helmet and pistol were still intact, as were Carson's soiled carbide-tie and left shoe.

The hosts didn't receive re-welcome applause. Instead, one audience member cried, "Hurry! Half the place is already gone!"

General Patton looked on in disgust as Jackie Gleason ate his way through the right-hand side of the studio audience; blood, intestines and bones flew through the air and into the abyss as if an oversized, unmanned wood chipper had been let loose.

"You fat sonofa—" Patton said as he squeezed off his last shot.

Gleason looked up in time to feel a warm breeze slap him between the eyes. The arm in his mouth fell to the floor. Blood spilled from his forehead.

The audience cheered when Gleason wobbled side to side, then tipped over the rear railing into wherever it was that waited below.

"Ladies and gentlemen, let's hear it for General George S. Patton!"

What was left of the crowd went wild. Patton walked among them. Some hugged him, some cried, but all saluted as he walked to the rear of the suspended studio, then back to his place next to Johnny.

"I can't remember the last time we've seen this much excitement around here," the band leader said from the side of the stage.

"That makes two of us," Johnny said, patting Patton on the back.

The seats that had been emptied by the obese closet-cannibal filled in, one at a time. When the studio audience was again complete, Johnny said, "Okay, folks. Our next guest is an old friend of the *Tomorrow Night Show* ... you know him, you love him ... the always funny Mr. Dom Deluise!"

As the second full-figured guest of Patton's tenure came toward the stage, Patton reached between the couch cushions and pulled out fresh ammo. He reloaded his pistol as he scanned the crowd, looking for the next one to step out of line.

INSIDE THE JIGGLES CAFE

Author's Note: This was written for an anthology of stripper-themed stories, but wasn't included due to a few unusual reasons. This was heavily influenced by the TV show Bar Rescue, and yes, the main protagonist here is inspired by the show's host.

From the outside, The Jiggles Café looked more like a small warehouse than an adult lounge. Its dirty white paint job flaked imitation stucco onto small patches of brown grass, giving the illusion of light snow. The parking lot needed serious re-paving, and God only knew what surprises were to be found behind the bar and in the kitchen.

Frank Millson sat in his SUV, taking in the establishment his brother had allowed to turn to shit. He had plenty of other business he should be attending to, and if not for having invested in the place three years ago, he'd gladly let his brother *and* the café rot.

At 10:04 a.m., Frank's brother arrived in an early '90s Toyota that appeared to be on its last leg. He pulled into a spot right by the front entrance. A trail of liquid spilled from the exhaust pipe; it continued dripping even after Steven shut off the engine.

"About time you showed up." Frank stepped out of his truck and slid on his sunglasses.

"Oh shit…I didn't even see you there!" Steven unlocked the front door, shut off the alarm, and then met his brother in the middle of the parking lot. "Thanks for coming, bro. I really appreciate it."

Frank shook his hand. It felt like the fat bastard had just consumed two glazed donuts on the ride in. "So tell me what's going on."

"Damn, bro. You don't waste any time, do you?"

"I think you've wasted enough time as it is." Frank walked by Steven and entered the Jiggles Café. *What a stupid fucking name*, he thought as he passed under the cheap sign, which Steven had ordered from some on-demand Internet printing company.

Frank had pleaded with Steven to think of a better name, but his brother was convinced it would draw the blue-collar crowd who worked in the nearby industrial town of Elizabeth, New Jersey. And while the place was successful for the first year, the Jiggles Café had rapidly turned into one of the most poorly -patronized strip clubs in the Garden State. Frank needed to do something about it before his investment was a complete loss and his brother started begging to live in his basement.

Despite no-smoking laws, the place reeked of dirty ashtrays. The bar itself needed replacing, and a new tap system was in order; there were only three beers on tap—Coors Light, Miller Lite and Bud—and each tap handle's logo had faded to an almost undecipherable splotch.

Frank walked behind the bar and began inspecting. Steven sat on one of ten stools and leaned over to watch.

"Seriously, Steven?" Frank held up a paper towel he'd used to wipe the Bud tap's nozzle. He winced at the brown-green stain smeared across it. "Do you smell this?"

Steven sat silent and shrugged his shoulders.

After wiping the other two nozzles, the paper towel fell apart. "Do you see this? *Do you?*" Frank threw the remains of the towel on the bar.

Slime splashed onto Steven's shirt, but he remained still. "No wonder no one comes here anymore. Would you?"

"We *do* have our regulars. At least, for the past month we have."

"*Regulars* aren't enough to get us out of this hole!" Frank picked up a shot glass, held it to the light, and noticed it had stains. He flung it at his brother's head. "And apparently having regulars for only a month hasn't helped too much, has it?"

"Actually, it has." Steven ducked. The glass nipped his left shoulder, then ricocheted to one of the five tables near the small stage.

It didn't break.

"Shut the hell up. Let's go," Frank said, pointing to the back of the club.

When they entered the kitchen, the amount of filth almost caused Frank to lose control. He pulled a metal basket out of the deep fryer. The grease was so thick it barely oozed from the holes, and chunks of black meat stuck to the basket's sides. He flung it into the wall next to the grill, which looked like it hadn't been wiped since the place opened. "You mean to tell me you assholes are actually cooking in here?"

"It's not always this dirty."

"Bullshit!" Frank opened one of the two refrigerators and almost threw up. He pulled one side of his jacket over his face and held up a bucket of uncovered, raw chicken wings. "This place is disgusting, and I'll bet any amount of money all your meat is bad. This fridge isn't even cold, let alone at standard temperature!" He threw the wings at Steven, who stepped out of the way. The polluted poultry splattered onto the floor. "No wonder no one orders food here like they used to! You're lucky no one has gotten sick or died from eating this shit!"

"Food isn't really what's been bringing the new regulars here," Steven said.

"No shit!" Frank went on to uncover two dead rats in the employee bathroom, cracks in the ceiling of the dancers' small dressing room, and so many other structural violations he had no idea how they hadn't yet been slapped with major fines.

When the inspection was done, Frank sat at the bar and pointed to the stool beside him.

Steven sat down, his face a mixture of embarrassment and exhaustion.

"So apparently we have a lot of work to do. Where the hell are your employees?"

Steven looked to the floor, then back at his brother, and said, "Willie won't be here for at least another hour, Stacy and Carmella should be here any minute, and Britney should be here any minute for the afternoon crowd."

"*Crowd?* How many people are usually here for lunch time?"

Steven looked to the floor for a second time. "Maybe two or three guys. But for a few weeks now, we've been getting about thirty people."

"I'll believe that when I see it!" Frank stood and walked over to the stage. "So I can assume all your money is being made on beer sales, correct?"

"Yep. And at night, the mixed drinks sell a bit better."

Frank laughed. He had no idea if his brother was even serious about this place anymore. "So your cook and two bartenders *knew* I was coming this morning, but none of them showed yet? Does your staff even give the slightest shit that they're about to be jobless if we can't fix this place?"

The front door opened and a tall brunette walked in. "Sorry I'm late, Steve. It took the cab forever to get to my apartment." She walked over and shook Frank's hand. "You must be Steve's brother. I'm Britney."

"Pleased to meet you," Frank said. *At least one of these morons showed up*, he thought.

When she walked to the dressing room, Steven said, "She's been our most popular dancer for the last month. If she ever leaves, we'll go under in no time."

Frank placed a toothpick in the side of his mouth. "She's definitely beautiful. But what's her deal?"

"What do you mean?"

"Why would someone so good-looking dance in a rat trap like this? She can't get work someplace better? Where I'm sure there are better tips?"

Steven laughed, then said, "Britney's talents aren't appreciated in other places. She appeals more to the working class crowd than the tight-assed snobs over in the city."

Frank rubbed his eyes, wondering if Britney's act was as bad as the condition of the club. "Well, can I *see* what's so great about her? Perhaps the entertainment won't need as much work as the rest of the place."

"Of course. Just grab a table and she'll be out in a few minutes."

Steven ran to a small booth beside the stage and put on some music. Frank could see he used an old CD player, but for some miraculous reason the sound wasn't too bad.

After Foghat's "Slow Ride" ended, Aerosmith's "Back in the Saddle" came on. Frank was pleased that his brother at least got the music right for his target audience. He needed to ask him if there was a regular DJ, or if he just played homemade compilations.

Britney eventually walked to the center of the small stage, acting as if the place was packed. She threw her bag to the side, then swung herself around the centered pole. Despite wearing a black bikini top and miniskirt, her long black gloves gave her a classier aura.

She did all the standard stripper moves, highlighted by a lot of the kind of butt-shaking that seemed to be the big thing lately. Frank never cared for it, but Britney's technique was hard not to admire.

Another classic rock track came on, but Frank couldn't remember the name or the artist. Britney began lip syncing along and stepped off the stage, approaching Frank. He kept his cool as she threw her left foot onto the side of his chair and gyrated her hips, giving him a slight peek at the side of her shaved crotch. She slowly removed one glove, turning her typical strip-joint act into a more burlesque-style performance. She pulled off the other glove, then gently tossed both onto Frank's lap.

Steven smiled from inside the small DJ booth as Britney removed her top, exposing two of the most perfect breasts Frank had ever seen.

"Hold it!" Frank said.

Steven stopped the music. "What's wrong?"

"What's wrong? Don't you know Jersey has a no-nudity law?"

Before Frank knew what hit him, Steven turned up the music louder and Britney pushed him back into his seat. She slid off her miniskirt and artfully twisted it behind his neck, pulling his head between her tits. But he pulled back, repulsed.

"Is this what goes on in here? You're lucky an undercover cop hasn't closed the place down yet—"

Frank stopped yelling as Britney took a step back and peeled off a strip of skin from her wrist to her elbow. A small amount of blood tapped onto the floor, but she didn't seem to be in any kind of pain. She peeled the strip of flesh next to it, and then did another three sections until her forearm's muscles were exposed like a pink banana. She did the same to her other arm, then peeled her skin from elbow to shoulder.

This has to be some kind of sideshow trick, Frank thought, not letting the disturbing sight get the best of him. He couldn't get over how real it looked, but there was no way someone could perform self-flagellation without crying out in agony. And Britney danced so well, he doubted she was on any serious painkillers or other substances.

Frank continued watching as she peeled and peeled, her skin coming off as if it were made of tissue paper. When her body had been completely de-skinned, Britney tugged her hair out a handful at a time. Each time she did, the club seemed to glow a different color, as if it was trying to highlight her act, but Frank knew the Jiggles Café had no kind of custom lighting. He began to wonder if his brother had slipped something into his drink. As Britney started digging into her midsection, Frank realized he hadn't had anything to eat or drink since breakfast, so whatever was happening wasn't an illusion—at least outwardly.

Britney stepped back onto the stage and began pulling her intestines out like a magician doing the old endless-handkerchief-from-the-palm trick. Her guts hit the floor with a sloppy sound, audible even over the blaring music.

"Okay, that's about enough of this bullshit," Frank said. But Britney hit him in the head with one of her organs—her liver, if he had to take a guess—so he sat back down, starting to worry that he might be having some kind of breakdown. And if he wasn't, how much longer could she disembowel herself before there was nothing left?

Frank was still convinced this was some insane trick, and he was about to rip the CD player out of the wall when the chicken wings he'd thrown at his brother hopped onto the stage and began dancing around Britney. They bopped in a circular motion as she continued pulling out her innards. The wings seemed to dance faster when she started tearing away her face muscles, exposing her cheekbone.

Frank looked on, doing his best to keep his cool and his patience. Something had to give. The trick had to be coming to a close, and then his brother had better have a good excuse why he wasted all this time on such a stupid prank.

Suddenly, every table was filled with men who looked to be somewhere between their late thirties and early fifties. Frank figured they must have wandered in during the commotion, and each one cheered in wild appreciation as Britney revealed more and more of her skeleton.

A heavy metal song started playing. Frank couldn't decide if he was feeling ill because of Britney's antics or because of the painfully grating music.

Britney had become a dancing skeleton within a few minutes, completely shed of skin, hair and organs, with the exception of her eyeballs.

Frank saw another woman walk to the dressing room as if nothing was wrong. He figured he'd go try to talk to her and see what was going on.

The crowd of men applauded and cheered the skeletal stripper as she worked the pole. Frank had no idea how she managed to stay in her high heels with no skin or muscle on her feet.

No one was in the dressing room or the employee bathroom. Frank decided to check the kitchen. Surely this woman had to be around somewhere.

Or... *maybe she was stealing and in cahoots with Britney, causing the place to go under even faster!* Yes, that had to be what was happening! Britney's insane act provided the perfect distraction, and Steven's office was just on the other side of the kitchen.

Frank entered the filthy cooking area. Grease was rising from the deep fryer, taking on a human-like form. The air was thick with a burned-food fog, even though no one had cooked in here yet today.

The woman he'd been pursuing came in from the office, noticed the fryer-grease man, and said, "Baby! About time you got here!" She threw her arms around the gelatin mass, and within seconds her entire body was inside it. She looked distorted, like someone behind a glass shower door, only darker. The mass oozed all over her, and Frank could tell she was kissing it by the way her eyes were closed; if anyone else walked in right now, they'd think she was trying to taste the glop rather than participate in some kind of obscure make-out session with it.

Frank walked back out to the stage area. Britney was still swinging around the pole, and he noticed one of her six-inch heels had finally fallen off. But the crowd continued cheering and the chicken wings continued dancing, and it appeared that one of the bartenders had finally arrived.

"Stacy?" Frank asked as he sat down at the bar.

"No, Carmella. Are you Steven's brother?"

"Yes. May I ask you a question, Carmella?"

"Of course," she said. She poured a beer from the Bud tap and handed it to a patron who'd managed to pry himself away from Britney's act for a few seconds.

"Would you mind telling me just what in the hell's going on here?"

"You mean Steven hasn't told you?"

"Told me what?"

"Britney's act has been bringing people back to Jiggles. She's been dancing here almost every day for the lunch crowd, then around ten o'clock for the night shift. She's awesome!"

Frank turned around on his stool and observed the audience. Britney and the chicken wings continued their routine, but there was something about the cheering men he couldn't quite put his finger on. They seemed like regular blue-collar workers, most likely from the surrounding industrial plants and businesses. And yet, they were going crazy for this show that would seem odd even in the trendiest artsy-fartsy club in Greenwich Village. Usually the blue-collar crowd wanted domestic beer, some fried burgers, and a big-titted dancer who didn't rip the skin from her bones.

The woman from the back room walked through the crowd, carrying a case of Heineken bottles. She placed them on the edge of the bar and said, "Be with you in a few," then grabbed a bar towel and wiped slime from her face as she returned to the back room.

"Can I assume that's Stacy?" Frank asked.

"That's her," Carmella said, taking the Heineken bottles out and placing them in a small fridge under the counter. "I'll introduce you when she comes back."

"Actually, we've already met," Frank said, thinking of her make-out session with the man-sized wad of grease.

Frank felt a tap on his shoulder. He turned around to see his brother standing there. "So, what do you think? In another couple of weeks, we should finally even out."

"Even out, huh?" Frank said. "And what makes you think you're not going to get caught having dancers go full-frontal, let alone ripping their skin off and whatever other crazy shit you're not telling me about?"

"Just trust me, brother," Steven said, taking one of the bottles from Carmella's hand.

Frank took the bottle back and put it on the bar. "I don't care how good you claim you're starting to do. *No drinking* while you're on the clock. You understand me?"

Steven stepped back and held his hands up in mock surrender. "Okay, okay." He turned and danced in place to the music as Britney got down on all fours. The chicken legs jumped, bounced off her spine, and then landed on the tables in front of the stage, where they continued dancing for the appreciative audience.

Frank took another count. There were now forty-seven men in the Café, almost twice as many as had been there only a few minutes ago.

Britney stood up and danced her way through the crowd. Crazed men tucked dollar bills into her ribcage and along her spine. She kissed one man who handed her a twenty-dollar bill, but to Frank it looked as if she were biting him, her face being absent of flesh and muscle. The man cheered and danced in place as Britney moved closer to the bar.

Frank turned around and decided he needed a drink. He ordered a Jack and Coke, which Carmella poured him with a smile. He didn't even bother inspecting the glass, which he figured was filthy. He just needed the alcohol in his system before anything else unusual happened.

"Compliments of the chef," Stacy said, handing Frank a platter containing a big, juicy cheeseburger and a side of thick-cut French fries.

"No offense, but I've seen the kitchen. I'm not eating anything that was cooked back there."

"Oh, come on, Frank." Stacy sat next to him and ate one of the fries. She nodded to the back room. "Willie's one of the best bar chefs in Jersey."

Frank turned and saw the man-sized mass of grease looking his way, holding his thumb up. "That's Willie?"

"That's Willie! Best cook around," Stacy said, then leaned in to Frank's ear and said, "And best lover I ever had."

Suddenly nauseated, Frank got up from his stool and made his way to the front of the Café. His brother was as enthralled with Britney's performance as the rest of the crowd. Stacy delivered drinks to packed tables, and Carmella poured more drinks like a seasoned professional. He also noticed every table was stacked with food. Frank had no idea how Willie could've cooked so much in such a short period of time.

When Frank stepped out into the parking lot, his two assistants had finally arrived. Chef Tom Huffy had driven down from Boston to lend his expertise in the kitchen; with him was expert mixologist Jason Rangle, who'd won the prestigious 2012 Bartender of the Year competition in Las Vegas.

Frank approached them and shook both their hands. "We have a very unusual situation here, boys."

Tom and Jason looked at each other.

"I've never seen anything quite like this." Frank motioned for them to follow him into the Jiggles Café.

They entered the bar, and Tom and Jason ran immediately onto the stage and began dancing with the skeletal Britney. Frank's mouth dropped open.

Tom got behind her and dry-hump danced while Jason took the front and did the same. It looked like a threesome from the most obscure adult video, and the place was even more crowded than when Frank had stepped outside just a few moments earlier.

Something's got to give, Frank thought. Jason left the threesome to be hoisted into the air by the crowd, which now seemed to be over seventy-five people strong. Jason sang along with the music as he was floated toward the bar. Carmella took the lid off an extra-large blender Frank hadn't noticed, and the crowd slid Jason into it as they, too, sang along to the song. When his body was inside, she slammed the lid back on and pressed a button. Frank could see Jason being ground to bits, but the mixologist's face showed no fear.

What it showed was absolute, otherworldly, appreciative pleasure.

Frank's first thought was to flee and get the first policeman he could find. But when he saw Tom walk into the kitchen area, he fought his instincts and decided to try saving his long-time colleague.

Making his way through the crowd was twice as difficult as before. The audience seemed to ignore him and his "Excuse me's," but Frank eventually made it to the kitchen.

"This guy's pretty good," Tom said, squatting over the grill and wearing nothing but his chef's shirt.

"Tom…what in the…"

Willie the human grease-man fried up Tom's excrement as it fell from his anus. Stacy came in and out, taking four plates at a time to the roaring crowd.

"That's it, Willie! That's it!" Tom continued pumping out chunks as the Jiggles Café chef flipped them and added seasoning with lightning agility. "Fantastic job!"

Frank peeked outside the kitchen. The crowd scoffed the burgers down so fast he had no idea how one chef was keeping up.

Britney and the chicken wings continued dancing as if they'd just started; as if they were robots, incapable of growing tired.

At the bar, Frank saw Carmella pouring his ground-up mixologist into martini glasses. Each time she rang one up, the cash register indicated $15.50.

Frank stepped behind the bar and looked at a couple of receipts. He noticed that as the crowd grew, they'd started charging double the price for their burger and fries platter. And since Tom had entered the kitchen, they charged triple, and the crowd seemed only too happy to pay the upped tab.

Frank ordered another Jack and Coke. Carmella made it for him, and it tasted even better than the first one. It was the first time he'd ever had a drink on the job, but he felt it was necessary given the current situation.

* * *

As he sat outside in his SUV, Frank Millson considered what he'd seen inside The Jiggles Café. He looked at the final tallies from the lunch crowd and couldn't wrap his head around the figure. Steven had made almost as much money in the past two hours as he had in the previous year.

His brother knocked on his window. "Are you okay?"

Frank looked at him and said, "I'm fine."

"So you think I'll be out of the hole soon?"

"If this keeps up," Frank said, holding up the lunchtime receipt, "I'm sure you will be."

"You mean you're sure *we* will be."

A cab pulled up to the front door and beeped. Britney came out—in her full flesh—and jumped in. As soon as she was gone, the crowd slowly dispersed.

"Thanks for coming down, brother. I hope it wasn't a waste of your time?"

Frank shook his brother's hand. "No. Not at all." He handed the receipt back to Steven. "Take care. And keep up the good work."

Steven smiled, then turned to head back to the Café. As he reached for the door handle, Frank called him.

"What's up?" Steven asked.

"I'll be back next week. Make sure that fucking kitchen is cleaned." Frank Millson then pulled out of the parking lot and tossed his toothpick out the window.

THE HUSBAND

Author's Note: While I'm a huge fan of twist endings, I hardly ever come up with any. I actually thought about the following story when I was a kid, maybe in fourth grade? I finally wrote this in the early 2000s but never submitted anywhere.

Jim Hardy jumped through the doors just as the train took off. He walked through the sweaty crowd, focusing on his balance.

He saw her midway into the car.

Surprisingly, the seat next to her was vacant.

Gorgeous. Hypnotizing eyes.

He sat down and rested the tan briefcase between his feet. Her beauty delayed his noticing her hair and clothing: vintage, 1930s style. She put her right hand on the seat in front of her.

No ring, Jeff thought. He built up enough courage, then spoke. "How are you doing?"

She looked at him. He was relieved by her polite, albeit rushed, response. "Okay. How about yourself?"

"Good, thank you."

Although taken aback by her beauty and out-of-date look, Jeff couldn't help but notice her constantly turning around as they chatted. Was someone following her?

As she spoke, he could have sworn he was in a time warp; he'd never met a woman so properly mannered in his forty-two years as a New Yorker.

When the train came to the next stop, the woman once again looked over her shoulder. Jeff changed his mind. He had to ask. "I hate to sound nosy, but is something wrong?"

"Yes," she said without hesitation. "It's my husband." A tear ran slowly over her cheek.

"I didn't mean to snoop—"

"No…no. It's all right. It's just—"

"It's just none of my business."

She grabbed his arm. "I hate him! I was forced into this marriage… it's such a long story."

"Is there anything I can do?"

"Oh, no," she said, wiping her tears with an old-looking handkerchief. "There's nothing anyone can do. It's just—I mean—I wish I could have met a nice gentleman like you sooner."

He hardly knew the woman, but Jeff Hardy was experiencing love at first sight. He wanted to kill whoever was making such a lovely, sweet woman so miserable.

"I'm sorry to unload this on you," she said, looking straight ahead.

"I just wish you'd let me help. Are you sure there's nothing I can—"

The train stopped short. People flew over Jeff and the woman's seats. The lights cut out. Jeff's head hit the hard seat in front of him, and he couldn't move. Blood ran from his forehead into his mouth. He watched the woman as she struggled for footing and tried to help him up. He couldn't hear a word she was saying.

The side of the car peeled open like a sardine can.

Jeff Hardy blacked out.

Less than a minute later, he regained consciousness. His heart pumped its final beats as he saw the woman being carried toward the Empire State Building by an unusually large ape.

I BURIED A FERGASON

(a.k.a. Zombie VIII in Italy)

Author's Note: There was an episode of Married With Children *where Al Bundy was SO thrilled he managed to find a vintage toilet called a Fergason, it was all he could think or talk about. The whole thing cracked me up, so when I wrote this toilet-themed story for a bizarro anthology, I knew I had to adopt the name. As for this story's subtitle? Before Google, zombie/cannibal film fans were always confused as re-titled movies would pop up all the time, causing double purchases and video rentals and unneeded aggravation. What does that have to do with a Fergason toilet? Pretty much nothing…*

One morning in early October, a loud flush startled Carl Washington from his sleep. He swatted at a fly as it landed on his bare chest, but he wasn't quick enough. He grunted at the self-inflicted sting.

Then came another sound, this time like a bucket of oatmeal being dumped into a pool.

Carl jumped into his overalls and went to check his mother, who was losing her breakfast thanks to a nasty case of East Nile Virus. "Ya awlright, maw?"

Rebecca Washington wiped her mouth, looking up at her six-foot, four-inch tall son. "Oh, I'll be awlright. Damn!" she said, looking down at her nightgown. "Another one ruint…unless I git'er in the washin' machine right away." She stood up and tore the nightgown off, running to the other side of the house she'd helped build thirty years ago with her late husband. Carl turned away to avoid seeing his mother naked. Considering the bathroom reeked of bacon and whiskey, Carl assumed she'd once again substituted Jack Daniels for Tropicana.

Carl looked away as he flushed the toilet, which was filled with a sickening yellow and brown glop. He felt an itching sensation, then swatted a huge bug and noticed the sucker had drawn blood—right from his neck. "Dang mosquitoes," he said, giving a second flush as he poured powdered Ajax in and around the toilet, scrubbing thoroughly with a worn bowl brush. "When're they gonna spray for that virus? When we all finally get it?"

Rebecca Washington had been diagnosed with East Nile Virus, a nasty little bug that caused high fever, temporary blindness, and a bad case of the shakes. She'd been dealing with it fine since Dr. Smith gave her the news last month, but Carl saw that things were becoming worse than the family doctor had told them.

Becky (as Dad used to call her) had been throwing up every day for the past week, sometimes two or three times, each instance worse than the last. Carl wondered if she'd remember to breathe if he wasn't around all the time to check on her.

"Dang!" Becky yelled from the washroom, the machine filling with water.

Carl walked in, watched his mother scrubbing her filthy nightgown, then headed outside to begin working. "You take it easy now, maw. 'Member what Dr. Smith told you."

Becky ignored him as he made his way to the barn. She dropped the soiled garment into the machine.

Despite the roar of the tractor, Carl could still hear his mother screaming at her nightgown—at her illness—and said a silent prayer as he headed out to the tobacco fields with a home-grown joint between his lips.

* * *

Carl gagged as he tried to read the paper. Even though he'd already cleaned the bathroom four times today, it still smelled of his mother's vomit. If bleach couldn't kill the stench, he wondered what could. He leaned up on the seat, checking around for anything he might have missed. But the bowl and the floor were spotless. Sparkling, even.

He tried making his way through the baseball standings, but couldn't.

He cleaned himself, flushed, then sat on the hamper, wondering what he was going to do. Callie Henlen was coming over tomorrow night, and although she understood he wasn't Donald Trump, he still wanted to make as good an impression as possible. He'd even managed to bribe Uncle Cletis, with the help of thirty-five bucks and a small bag of weed, to watch Mom over at his house for the night so he'd have some privacy.

Mom was sleeping soundly, a blessing these days, giving Carl some time to go out to the barn. He looked around back, behind some old bikes, rakes, and drop cloths.

"Awl-right!" he said, thrilled that he never got rid of the old but unused toilet bowl. His father had planned to install it in the barn a few weeks before his untimely death. It had been sitting out here ever since, protected by a thick black garbage bag.

Carl went back to the house, grabbed an eighteen-inch monkey wrench from under the sink and headed to the bathroom, where he again found his mother puking her guts out. "Maw! You awlright?"

"'Course…I ain't…awlright…ya dernt fool!" She heaved another mass of chunks into the bowl before passing out.

Carl dragged her to the side, checked her pulse, then covered her with a towel. He flushed the mess, did his Ajax routine, mopped the floor, and began to disassemble the stench-spewing toilet.

He picked up the wrench after shutting off the feed valve. The sound of the wrench clanging off the tiled floor rejuvenated his mother.

"Just what in the hell you think yer doin'?"

"What does it look like, maw? I'm getting rid of this stinkin' thing."

"Like hell you are!"

Becky stood up, looking like she was about to hurl, then spoke again. "You can't get rid of that! They don't make Fergasons anymore, you jackass!"

"So what, maw? We've got another one out in the barn that don't smell nothin' like this…"

"Don't you be touchin' nothin'," she said, reaching for the heavy wrench.

"Maw, are you outta your mind?" Carl pulled the wrench from her hands. "This house stinks to high heaven, and I gots a date comin' over tomorrow night! I clean and I clean and I clean and the thing still stinks!"

"Lemme show you what you're doin' wrong," she said, dumping the Ajax all over the bowl. She missed, covering herself and the floor with the white powder.

"Come on, maw! Look what yer doin'!"

"Oh, keep quiet, son. Lemme show ya' how to clean the Fergie!"

And then she passed out—if from the powdered bleach or the East Nile, Carl didn't know—but he knew he had very little time to change the toilet.

He carried his mother back to bed, then removed the Fergason from the Washington household. Within a half hour, he managed to take it out to the barn, install the other one, and clean up the mess.

The place smelled better already.

* * *

"It's no big deal, maw," Carl said, walking his mother back up the steps. He'd taken her out to see that the Fergason was okay when she became extremely nauseous. "Just remember to do yer business right out the back door."

Becky walked, leaning on his arm, looking worse than ever.

"Just try 'n remember I dug the hole right under there," he said, pointing to a lawn chair at the bottom of the back steps. "Long as you come out here when yer sick, the house'll stay nice and clean."

"I'll try, son, but I don't like the Fergie bein' out in the barn. Your paw and me put that sucker in before any of the walls were even up," she said, her voice cracking. "It was our special…"

"Please, maw! Don't go tellin' me no stupid toilet bowl is what reminds you of paw! That's downright wrong!"

Becky slapped her son across the face with her bony hand. It hurt, but Carl kept his composure. "The Fergie's no stupid toilet bowl, ya heffer-assed imbecile! The Fergie was the most sought-after bowl back then, and yer paw broke his back to git us one."

Carl opened the back door but kept his silence, remembering the preacher's sermon a few weeks ago about honoring your parents. He tried—God knew he tried—but there was no way that smelly thing was staying in the house with Callie comin' over tonight. He said a silent prayer, then propped his mother in front of the television.

"Uncle Cletis should be here in a little while, maw. You's are gonna have a great time tonight."

"We're playin' cards, right?"

"Yep. I made sure to remind him to get a new deck, and I'm sure Aunt Martha will sit in on the game."

"That old goat? I don't think she could even see the dang cards no more!"

Carl laughed, happy to see his mother smiling for the first time in a week. "I'll be inside in a bit, maw. *Oprah*'s startin' in a few minutes."

Becky had vomited all over the back of the barn, hitting the Fergason before Carl had a chance to re-cover it with the heavy black bag. He was heading out to clean when he heard Uncle Cletis' horn beep.

Carl wondered what he was doing there so early.

By the time he had his mother in the car with all her medicine and changes of clothes, Carl had forgotten all about cleaning the old Fergason. By the time he showered, threw two steaks on the grill, and prepared the home-grown vegetables, Callie was knocking on the door.

* * *

Carl couldn't read Callie. She said she loved the meal and enjoyed their conversation. But when he put his arm around her on the couch, she stood up and said she didn't realize how late it was, and how she had to get up early tomorrow for work at the town pharmacy. Perhaps it was just nervousness? Or maybe he said something that turned her off? He thought hard on their time together and couldn't figure it out.

But she did promise another date...and she'd given him a kiss on the cheek for walking her down to the car.

Carl decided he was okay with the way the night turned out, until Uncle Cletis called and said Maw was staying the night. She had passed out after sneaking a little too much moonshine, which didn't mix too well with the meds she was taking for the East Nile. So now he had the whole house to himself, and no woman to share it with.

Then that hated scent drifted in the window, turning Carl's attention and stomach away from thoughts of Callie Henlen. He grabbed a flashlight and went out to the barn. The puke had hardened to the Fergason, creating a brutal stench like no other.

"You're a real idiot, y'know that, Carl?" He covered his nose with the bottom of his flannel shirt. "What am I gonna do now?"

And that was when he spotted his shovel leaning against the wall.

"Of course," he said, tipping the bowl onto a thick drop-cloth. He dragged it out to the middle of the tobacco field, right next to the area where he harvested his own stash.

By the light of the October moon, Carl Washington removed his shirt and dug into the hardening soil. His biceps bulged. He was unaware that most men would kill to have his physique—one that came naturally, thanks to long hours of hard labor.

Carl didn't rest until the final shovelful of earth was patted down. The Fergason was now six feet deep in his property's most secluded section, never again to annoy anyone with its smell.

After catching the sports on the local nightly news, Carl fell asleep on the couch, praying for his mother, and that Callie would keep her promise for a second date.

* * *

"Are you sure this place is cool?"

"Yeah…what if that inbred finds us partying on his property? He'll probably barbeque us or something."

"Oh, please," Jason Henlen said. "He's a bigger geek than my sister! He wouldn't hurt a fly."

"I'd hate to mess with him, though," said someone in the gathering crowd.

"Listen, everyone," Jason said, shining the flashlight on his face. "We've got plenty of weed, plenty of brew and plenty of tunes. If anyone wants to split, go right ahead. If not, let's stop the crying and get down to business!"

Everyone shouted in approval, then began stepping over the useless fence dividing the Washington property from the outskirts of Creekville. It took a while to reach the middle of the tobacco field, but when they did, the rave was on: a small boom box blared techno music through an area unaccustomed to anything other than country and bluegrass. Beer spilled, joints were lit, and non-dancing couples snuck off in all directions to fool around.

Jason tripped on something, caught a few laughs from the stoned crowd, then realized what had happened. "What the—"

He fished his flashlight from his back pocket and illuminated a large plant—or was it some kind of tree? Someone turned off the music, and within seconds everyone was staring where Jason's light was aimed.

"Sweet Moses! Is that what I think it is?"

Jason stuck his foot before the plant, which easily stretched twenty feet into the air. How had no one noticed this during the long trek in? The earth surrounding the growth was freshly turned over. The plant was dark green, covered from base to top with thick, fuzzy, yolk-yellow leaves.

Jason took a whiff of it. His eyes opened as if he'd stuck his finger in an electrical socket. "I think this Washington freak's on to something here—come smell this sucker!"

The ravers began pulling off the leaves, smelling and tasting—eventually, a few people hacked up the moist leaves with razor blades, adding the blend to their joints.

A woman handed Jason a blunt full of the freshly chopped weed. It had seemed to dry as she chopped it, unusual for any kind of plant.

"I guess I'll be the first," Jason said, whipping out his Zippo. Once lit, the smell turned disgusting, but he took a toke. He coughed and took another. Then he screamed, "Come get your *Washington Tree*! YEE-HAR!"

The huge joint went around. Everyone who took a puff was instantly flying high.

The ravers stuffed their pockets with the Washington Tree leaves, a few of them sitting on the side and rolling more mammoth joints.

The music came back on. Girls tossed off their shirts as they danced; the guys were too wasted to realize what they were doing.

Jason hoped the high would stop here, now that one of the topless girls appeared to be melting. That Hawaiian stuff gave some brief hallucinations, but this was different. His arms started going lukewarm, then hot, and before he knew it, Jason found himself dumping a forty-ounce Budweiser over his head to cool off.

"Yo, dude—what's your problem?"

"I'm burning up," Jason said, trying not to sound panicked.

"Haha! Yeah! Me too," some guy said, who followed suit with another forty.

The music abruptly stopped as the boom box was blown to pieces.

* * *

Everyone stared at the hulking figure standing atop a running tractor.

"Now just who the hell are y'all?" Carl Washington said, aiming his shotgun at the crowd of teenagers. "And what're y'all doing on my property?"

No one answered.

Jason fell on the ground and started twitching.

"What's wrong with yer friend there?" Carl asked, shining his flashlight on the convulsing partier.

"I-I don't know," one of the girls said. "We didn't do nothing wrong, sir. We're just having a few beers."

"And smoking some of your weed—great stuff you got here!" one of the guys said, right before falling down and joining Jason in wild twitch-mode.

Carl sat back down on his tractor, shotgun aimed at the convulsing crowd. It looked like the teenagers had planted some kind of huge tree right where he'd buried the Fergason a few hours ago.

He wondered what was happening to them. Yellow bile spilled from their mouths; everyone ripped off their clothing, sweating blood and drops of red-green pus.

Carl backed up the tractor, wondering if those idiots in government had finally sprayed for the East Nile and wound up killing more than mosquitoes. He wrapped a bandanna around his face, trying not to breathe whatever was in the air.

The teenagers continued twitching on the ground. One stood and started walking toward the tractor.

"What in the name of a rattler's ass?"

One by one, the convulsing teens stood and followed the first to rise. They walked like drunken mummies, dragging their feet, arms forward as if trying to keep their balance. The eerie sounds coming from their mouths chilled Carl to the bone. He backed up as fast as possible before spinning around and flooring it to the barn.

He ran into the house, locked both doors, and climbed up to the roof. He could see them trailing through the rows of tobacco, heading straight for him, but he had a while until they would arrive. Carl decided to run down to the kitchen and call Uncle Cletis. Surely he'd know more about this than Carl did, being a Vietnam veteran and all.

* * *

"What took you so long, Uncle Clee?" Carl asked, opening the front door. He let his uncle in and then quickly locked up behind him.

"I had to make sure your aunt knew I was coming over."

A loud crash alerted them.

"They must be near the barn," Carl said, leading Cletis up to the roof. The sun was starting to show, spraying the Washington property with much-needed light.

"Now just what on earth's wrong with those kids?" Cletis asked, looking down at his nephew's back yard.

"I was hopin' you could tell me. I heard them makin' all kinds of racket out in the field—bastards woke me up—and when I got out there, they was all flippin' and floppin' on the ground like a bunch of catfish."

Cletis removed his sweat-stained baseball cap.

"What is it, Uncle Clee?"

Cletis put a hand on his nephew's shoulder. "I saw something just like this in 'Nam." He sat on the roof and pulled a small handgun from his pants. "This is bad...very bad."

"What is?" Carl asked. His anger rose as he watched a teenager fall into the puke-hole he'd dug for his mom.

"This is sorta what happened that time right outsida' Ho-chee-man city. This is why they invented napalm!" Cletis stood up and started shooting at the teenagers. Carl quickly grabbed his uncle's gun.

"Whoa! Hold on there! Are you havin' another flashback?"

Cletis started crying, then quickly stopped and took his gun back. "No, I'm not, son. But those bastards are gonna rip us apart if we don't stop 'em!"

"What?"

"Are you listening to me, Carl? Take them down, now!"

"But..."

"I said now, soldier!"

Without further hesitation, Carl followed Cletis in shooting down the yard full of convulsing teenagers. He noticed they'd brought the smell of the Fergason with them, which intensified each time one of them was blown apart.

He recalled a story his uncle had told about one of his tours in 'Nam, when a village of allegedly starving Vietnamese had attacked someone in the platoon, tearing him to pieces and eating him alive. Without hesitation, the cannibals were torched with napalm, and his patrol was quickly quarantined for a week until each of them had received several blood tests.

"That's when we all realized them folk weren't really starving," Uncle Cletis had said, ending his story in a cold sweat. Carl began to wonder what kind of chemical, what kind of toxin... what kind of *weapon* had Uncle Sam been experimenting with over there?

He also began wondering if Uncle Sam was using the same chemical now against the East Nile.

"No, no, no! You gotta hit 'em in the head—blow 'em clean off! Trust me, son. I was killin' these gooks when you was still in your diapers!"

Within minutes, the Washington backyard became home to a pile of rotted, smelly teenaged potheads. A yellowish steam rose from their bodies, causing Carl and Cletis to gag. They went inside, filled their nostrils with VapoRub and covered their faces with bandannas, then went out to the backyard to assess the damage. There had to be a hundred of them, if not more.

"Looks like we've got a lot of work to do."

"Huh?" Carl said. "It looks like the dang *government* has a lot of work to do. I'm calling 'em as soon as..."

"Are you crazy, boy? If they's the one's who gone an' done this, they'll probably get rid of us, too. Just in case!"

Carl thought about it and agreed. "How're we supposed to get rid of 'em, then?"

"Well, we ain't got no napalm." Cletis turned to the tractor. "Follow me."

* * *

It took over two hours, but Carl managed to plow all the bodies into a section of his property where little tobacco grew. The plan was to douse them with gas and hope all the evidence burned up.

Carl wondered if it was the insecticide or the virus itself that transformed the kids. Would his mother end up like this? Had anyone else in town turned into one of these things yet?

Cletis helped Carl pour gas over the corpses. Carl tossed a match, and the field lit up like the Fourth of July, despite the fact the sun was now shining.

"Hot dang! Looks like we've done it!" Cletis said, tucking his gun back into his belt.

But then the burning bodies stood and began convulsing even faster than before.

"For the love of Aunt Martha," Carl said, jamming shells into his shotgun. "Some of them ain't even got their heads!"

The reanimated bodies sensed the living and attacked. Carl and Cletis fled through rows of tobacco, the burning corpses moving faster than before.

"Follow me," Carl said, firing a blind shot behind them. They heard a couple of bodies hit the ground with a thud.

They came to the clearing that housed Carl's secret crop, the patch of earth that served as the Fergason's burial ground. They stopped by the huge tree, catching their breath.

"What in God's name is that?" Cletis asked, looking up at the strange growth.

"I have no clue," Carl said, taking aim at the path they'd come from. "I think these kids planted it or something."

The burning, hyper-spastic teens emerged from the wall of crop. Carl and Cletis took down as many as they could, too tired to keep running, then collapsed on opposite sides of the great tree.

The earth rumbled. Carl and Cletis scrambled back for safety.

The teenagers stopped, shaking. The tree tipped over, crushing a few of them dead.

"Come on, boy! The dang thing fell, is all! Keep firing!"

Carl joined his uncle, cutting the burning teenagers in half, wondering why the flames didn't eat them up.

Both men ran out of ammo.

Teenagers kept coming, some headless, some legless and pulling themselves forward with their arms. Those who still had eyes wore wicked stares.

Carl grabbed his aging uncle around the waist, attempting to carry him as long as he could.

The earth trembled again, dirt spraying from the place where the tree once stood, where the Fergason was buried.

Only it was buried no more.

Carl turned and stood motionless as the Fergason rose up from its grave. The toilet slid forward, its puke and dirt-covered seat rising.

One by one, the reanimated teenagers were drawn into the bowl. Their fires fizzled out as they plunged into its putrid waters. Carl and Cletis covered their ears from the sounds of crunching bones. For almost an hour, raver after raver fell into the Fergason: their evil flames extinguished, their lust for death eliminated, their bodies no more, sucked back into the dimension that had created them.

* * *

Two months later, Rebecca Washington and her son sat in the backyard, sipping lemonade and smoking a spliff of homegrown grass. Uncle Cletis flipped chicken legs on the grill. His face still showed sadness over the recent loss of his wife.

"If I'da known this shit was this good fer ya, I'da been smokin' it for years!" Becky said. She inhaled deeply, leaning her head back on the aged lawn chair, paying no mind to the puke-hole across from them. "Too bad we couldn't get some of this to Martha sooner."

Carl kissed his mother on the forehead before filling her glass. He was thankful for her new-found health, for his Uncle Cletis' guidance in eliminating those poor teenagers, and that only a few concerned parents had come around his property, asking if he'd heard anything about them. They'd each left convinced that Carl Washington had nothing to do with the disappearances.

Rebecca smiled, unaware that her son and brother-in-law had prevented a potential apocalypse. She was happy to rest next to their backyard décor's latest addition. She was unconcerned by how disturbing it might look to the neighbors.

The Fergason stood proudly in its new spot between the clothes line and cement bird bath, still in the process of forgiving Carl, but happy to be part of the Washington family again.

SHOP TIL YOU DROP

Author's Note: This one, featured in a Christmas-themed anthology, might be a bit too darkly humorous in light of recent events. It's obviously an absurd look at how ridiculous holiday shopping has become, but I still think it's a fun tale which, like most of my writing, was inspired by exploitation cinema.

Maryanne Nettles pulled into the Toy World parking lot and found a spot near the main entrance.

The 4:00 a.m. line was already wrapped around the building, so she assumed the vacant space must belong to someone who left in an emergency. Good. Her chances of obtaining a Robosaurus just went up a notch.

Approaching the line, the only sound she heard was a plow pushing snow into the center of the lot, creating an artificial mountain. It looked pretty despite its location in the suburban strip mall, which Maryanne hated patronizing unless absolutely necessary; but to please her precious little Johnny, neither snow nor long lines mattered.

The man in front of her shivered, underdressed in a light fall jacket.

What the hell's wrong with people? Christmas is only two weeks away,

Maryanne thought as she lit a cigarette. She felt under each arm to make sure she'd remembered everything. After disappointing her son last year, there was simply no way she was leaving without a Robosaurus. Her son's tears had haunted her all year long; the previous hot item, the similar Robomals, sold out in every brick and mortar store and online outlet. His heart had been set on the Robomal Gorilla, but the best she could do was a cheap knock-off, the name of which escaped her (*Gorillabot? Apedroid?*), and she couldn't even find one until his birthday in June.

Since August, the television commercials for the Robosaurus had aired relentlessly, and little Johnny's *only* wish was for one of the fifteen-inch-tall remote-controlled dino-bot hybrids.

And come hell or high water, he was going to unwrap one on Christmas morning.

Toy World was slated to open at 6:00 a.m. The crowd was growing restless by 5:35 as they saw employees jostling around through the front windows. A truck pulled alongside the line and opened its side, displaying buttered rolls, bagels, and a variety of coffee and tea. Of course, those who were there alone wouldn't risk leaving the line or even asking the person behind to hold their spot, but those who came in teams fueled up as the opening drew near.

5:55. Maryanne crouched and felt alongside each leg and her left inner thigh. She knew she was fully strapped, but it never hurt to make sure. Behind her, the line had grown by another three dozen people, and she estimated triple that number before her. *Shit*, she thought, thinking her boss would be the first one to pay if she didn't leave Toy World with a Robosaurus. The bastard had made her work a double shift yesterday, and by the time she got home, cooked for Johnny and caught a few winks, she had already been late. She knew midnight was the time most people began getting in line, but she just couldn't help the situation.

As the front doors finally opened, Maryanne went over her plan.

The long leather trench coat she'd owned since high school still fit perfectly, and the feel of the enforcers against her flesh was as reassuring as it was erotic. Her patience grew slim as she followed Mr. Shivers and the line of unworthy assholes in front of him.

When she entered the building, a blast of heat put her in a mild state of shock. She quickly refocused and headed to the left side, where Toy World kept action figures and similar goodies that appealed to young boys.

She unzipped her jacket a bit; her chest shone with sweat in the heat. Her long, thin red hair flew behind her as she picked up the pace.

She could see the Robosaurus logo from three aisles away. It hung from the ceiling above a pile of boxes, which were being consumed like meat chunks in a piranha pool.

Bastards. Bastards. Bastards.

When she arrived at the Robosaurus display, there were about twenty people fighting over the remaining stock. She remembered her son's face nearly a year earlier, and all but wept. That simply wasn't going to happen again. She slid her right hand under her left arm and felt the cold steel handle. But before she drew, a hole opened. Only a few people reached for the last five boxes, and one was easily within her grasp.

The freshly buffed floor helped her boots glide to the prize.

A genuine Robosaurus was now in Maryanne Nettles' possession. Her little Johnny was going to be the happiest kid on the planet in a couple of weeks, and she'd forever be his hero.

She turned to head to the checkout line.

"Where the hell do you think you're going, bitch?"

Maryanne had hoped she wouldn't have to go to extremes. She hoped the morons at Toy World would have ordered enough supply to fill the demand. But even as she grabbed the final Robosaurus, she had that certain feeling things had gone a bit too easy.

"Hand it over," a tall man with a long knife said. "Now." His two friends also drew blades, staring her down.

Well, I tried, she thought as she pulled her Glock 22 from her shoulder holster. "You sure you still want this?"

The man lunged, but Maryanne put the first round between his eyes, the second and third into his buddies' chests.

Everyone in the store turned toward the action figure area. Those with Robosauruses remained in line but ducked, protecting their precious gifts; customers took cover as they entered the store. Another man stepped out from behind an Amazing Spider- Man display. He drew his own Glock—to Maryanne it looked like an older model than hers—and fired.

Maryanne dashed down the aisle adjacent to the empty Robosaurus stand; the bullet sailed past her, piercinge the neck of a woman who'd been sneaking up on her with an aluminum baseball bat.

Maryanne reached the end of the aisle and looked up to see Glock Man coming after her. The bat-wielding woman was sprawled on the floor; the blood gushing from her neck caused a man to slip and knock over a display of *Star Wars* vehicles.

The man fired wildly, but Maryanne managed to catch his kneecaps with a quick spray from her second piece, an Uzi carbine she'd stolen from her ex-boyfriend. The man fell to the ground and dropped his pistol, screaming in agony.

Maryanne kicked in a door labeled *Employees Only* and ran down a long, narrow hallway, until she found a room where she could recover from the excitement. She eventually caught her breath and removed her jacket to cool off. She stuffed the Robosaurus into her son's backpack, which she then slung over her arms. She caught her breath and walked back up the narrow hallway. Surprisingly, no one had come after her.

With Glock and Uzi in hand—plus three backup pistols strapped to her legs—Maryanne Nettles kicked open the *Employees Only* door and began her trip to the checkout counter.

At first, she'd anticipated being swarmed. But as she peered down the aisles where Glock Man still lay crying, it seemed as if everyone was either hiding or had left.

"Come on out, bitches. You think you're going to fuck up my son's Christmas again this year? *Think again.*"

A canister flew by her head and nailed the door behind her. Maryanne saw the man who had hurled it coming from her left. She spun and placed a quick round of Glock goodness into his chest, sending him down like the bag of shit he was.

When nothing else flew toward her, she cautiously made her way up the aisle, stepping over Glock Man, who tried in vain to grab her. She thought of her son's disappointed face last Christmas as she kicked the man's hand, sending him into another round of screams.

Her black t-shirt and jeans were now stained with both Glock Man and Canister Man's blood, but she ignored it and continued to the checkout area.

Halfway there, a group of four women jumped her from behind. One took her Glock as another took her Uzi, but both were too stupid to realize the locks were on. Maryanne quickly pulled a 9x19mm Grandpower K100 from her inner thigh and shot both women dead. The two remaining women took a step back.

"Bunch of tough bitches?"

"No, we just—"

"You just what? Wanted to help destroy my son's Christmas like all these other assholes?"

"No, we just—"

"Bite me." Maryanne Nettles fed mouthfuls of bullets to the two would-be thieves, turning the backs of their heads to fine mist. She recovered her Glock and Uzi and re-strapped the Grandpower to her thigh.

"Hold it right there!"

Apparently she hadn't been cautious enough. The adrenaline rush of her first killings had obscured her senses. This time the end of a double-barrel shotgun rested against her temple. A tall, burly man in a blue Toy World vest held it steady.

"Drop your guns or your head becomes mush."

Maryanne did as she was told.

"Now drop the ones you have on your legs."

Shitshitshitshitshit. Think, Mary, think. Maryanne again pictured her son's disappointed face.

"Now," the man said, pressing the hard steel into her head.

"Okay…just give me a second to loosen the straps."

The man took a step back as Maryanne dropped the backpack and removed her black t-shirt. Her breasts now faced him at full attention.

"I said lose the guns, not your clothes—"

"They're all connected, asshole. I have to get my shirt off in order to…"

She had the schmuck right where she wanted him. His eyes remained transfixed on her tits as she babbled on, giving her just enough time to pull the Grandpower from her thigh and shoot his crotch at point-blank range. He dropped the shotgun. It fired and barely missed hitting Maryanne's right foot. Blood fell from between the man's legs. Maryanne figured he was in too much shock to scream; he fell in silence.

The checkout lanes were abandoned. No employees could be seen, so she assumed they had fled or were hiding. Maryanne stood by the first checkout lane, waiting for another customer challenge or irritating store-hero to come calling. After a few minutes, she decided the coast was clear.

She put her t-shirt back on and re-fastened the backpack. Snow fell lightly as she made her way to her car. She realized there were only a few other cars in the lot, and assumed she had scared most of their owners away.

In the distance, she could hear the snow plow doing its thing. She heard the wail of police sirens, and knew she'd better get out of there as quickly as possible.

And as she drove home, she could also hear the happiness of her son's voice when he opened the Robosaurus come Christmas morning.

ANARCHY CAFE

Author's Note: In 1986 I went to see GG ALLIN AND THE NY SUPERSCUM at the now defunct Cat Club in NYC. It was the sickest thing I've ever seen, and GG himself claimed it was the "Second sickest gig I ever did." If you don't know anything about GG Allin, he was a punk rock singer from New Hampshire who fronted many bands, and while he started out as a typical punk band in the late 70s, in the 80s his lyrics took on all forms of obscene ideas. His stage shows were insane, and often caused his sets to be cut within the first 3–4 songs. When I found out an anthology was going to be dedicated to bizarre stories dealing with GG, I nearly had a stroke. To be included in 'Blood For You, a Literary Tribute to GG Allin' was as surreal as it gets. In my story, I dealt with why GG's penis is so damn small…

New Hampshire, early 1985

It started as soon as he left her apartment.

If he hadn't known better, GG would have sworn a hamster was running amuck in his penis. He pushed down on the bulge in his pants, but the uncomfortable sensation wouldn't go away. And although this wasn't an erection, his junk seemed to grow with every step he took.

Amanda had called him for a reverse booty call, and GG was more than happy to oblige. He'd never been in such a dark apartment, and while it didn't bother him at the time, he was now suspicious about the countless inverted crosses and pentagrams decorating her walls, not to mention the sea of burning candles.

But what a good fuck she was. She banged him every which way but loose, and thinking about her made him temporarily forgot about the strange sensations currently running through his dick.

By the time he was five blocks from his pad, his member had grown large enough to rip through his zipper, requiring him to carry it the rest of the way with both arms, as if hauling a coffin.

Somehow GG made it to his apartment with minimal weird stares. His brother Merle was in front of the TV, jamming something on his unplugged electric guitar.

"We've got problems," GG said.

"What's that?" Merle asked. He must've been on something stronger than weed, because it took a minute for him to recognize his own brother.

"I said we've got problems." GG let go of his dick, which he'd been holding to his chest since leaving Amanda's. It slammed down on the makeshift coffee table, knocking Merle's ashtray and beer cans to the floor.

Merle stood and pulled his guitar over his shoulder. "What the fuck happened to you?"

"That bitch, that's what happened."

Merle laughed. He pointed at GG's swelled cock and laughed harder. A minute or two passed.

When he didn't calm down, GG said, "Enough already, asshole." His penis, as if of its own accord, swung out and smacked Merle in the side of the head, sending a couple of teeth flying to the carpet. GG could swear the dingus grew another several inches.

Merle finally stopped laughing. "All right! All right. Take it easy, fuckface." He took a sip from a fallen beer can and spit some blood on the floor. "You mean to tell me banging Amanda caused this?"

"Looks that way," GG said, sitting on the couch. His dick now stretched four feet past his legs and was almost twice as thick as his body.

"Damn. We've gotta do something about this."

"No shit, dickless." GG took the bandanna off his head. "Can you get me a beer? My mouth's dry as shit."

Merle went to the kitchen and returned with a Pabst tall boy. GG drained it in four gulps.

His schlong grew even longer and thicker.

Merle sat across from him and gawked.

"Staring at it isn't going to do anything," GG said.

"Shhhh. I think I've got an idea."

* * *

One of the bouncers dragged an unruly patron through the crowd and out the entrance. When the drunken fool refused to calm down, the bouncer lifted him by the throat and slammed him to the pavement, causing his body to split into countless butterfly-like creatures and sputter away. The people waiting in line continued talking, unaffected.

When the dismissed patron's friend came out looking for him, the bouncer lifted the rope and allowed two more people inside.

Merle flicked a cigarette butt halfway across the street. "Everything okay?"

"Everything's fine," the bouncer said, crossing his arms and staring at the endless line of night clubbers.

"Thanks." Merle went back inside. After witnessing Joe's method of dealing with trouble, he realized he'd picked the right man for the job.

He made his way through the long, cylindrical club, looking for his brother. The place was so packed he almost worried they'd run out of beer or whatever mixed drink everyone was sipping. The dance floor was jammed with people grinding up against each other, some having sex as if no one was watching, others laughing, yelling into each other's ears to hear over the deafening mix of punk, techno and industrial music.

A couple of girls gave Merle the eye, knowing he was co-owner of this fine establishment, but he kept on. He looked at the ceiling, which dripped with red and white liquid that never seemed to hit the floor. Its darkly fluorescent texture gave the entire place a dim glow.

A small group surrounded GG backstage, offering various drugs. The Scumfucs weren't due on stage for another half hour. Merle hoped the fire department wouldn't shut them down before the show, or at least until they sold every copy of their latest seven-inch single—although at this point, the cover charge would more than foot the bill for their next few recording sessions.

"So, GG," a young woman with spiky green hair asked. "What's the big surprise tonight?"

"You'll have to wait like everyone else," GG said, sticking his hand down the front of her tight jeans. The girl leaned back and enjoyed the probing as she toked a joint.

"Are you done fucking around yet?" Merle hated to interrupt, but business was business. "I gotta talk to you."

He pulled GG away from the girl and noticed the hand that GG had stuffed down her pants was now rainbow-colored.

GG sniffed it as he entered the small room they used as an office.

"What's so important?"

Merle lit another smoke and wiped the sweat from his forehead. "In the last half hour, the place has expanded by five feet."

"So? Tell Joe we can let more people in."

"That's just it. We'll have to call the fire department to change our occupancy sign. If they pull a surprise inspection, we'll be fucked."

GG laughed and took his pants off. He stood in black engineer boots, a dirty jock strap, and sleeveless dungaree jacket. "When the fuck did you become such a dick?"

"Someone has to keep things on the up and up around here. If we keep letting things slip, we'll be closed down before we know it."

"Will you relax?" GG slid on a pair of sunglasses. "Let me get through this gig. Then we'll deal with this bullshit. Okay?"

Merle spat on the floor and took a drag of his cigarette. "Fine."

When GG left to join his band, Merle sat on a ripped old couch they'd found in a strip mall parking lot and wondered when the hell he'd become so responsible. Perhaps it was when the cash started rolling in just two weeks after they opened the Anarchy Café. Or maybe it was when his brother had accepted what had happened to him and decided to deal with shit as long as he could, and so far he seemed to be dealing with things just fine.

Before Merle could worry any more, one of the walls widened at least a foot, filling the small room with a salty stench that made him gag. *At this rate*, he thought, *this place will take up half of New Hampshire in another month.*

* * *

During the third song of the Scumfucs' set, the green-haired girl from the back room jumped on stage and sang along with GG. Merle laughed from the back of the club, knowing she was in for it. And within seconds, GG ripped her shirt off and began fondling her tits.

But the girl was no pushover. As the crowd went wild, slam- dancing and singing along to "I Wanna Fuck Your Brains Out," she managed to tug down GG's jockstrap.

The crowd quickly became silent, and within a few moments, the band did too. For a moment, GG's gravelly voice was the only audible sound in the room; then he clued into everyone's silence.

Merle saw the whole crowd staring at his brother's crotch.

GG looked down.

The topless girl stood with her mouth wide open.

A goat head with glowing red eyes protruded from the spot where GG's cock should've been. Smoke gushed from its nose, and Merle felt the walls of the club expanding again. This time they seemed to stretch out at least five feet on all sides, pulsing blue veins and hairs like barbed wire jutting from every inch like morbid decorations.

Merle saw Joe admitting more and more people through the entrance and wondered if the goat head wasn't somehow communicating with both his brother and the bouncer.

As if there'd never been any silence, the band ripped back into the third verse. The crowd began raping each other, and Merle ran to the front to see what was going on with Joe.

"It's all cool," he said as Merle approached.

"What's all cool?"

"This. The Club. We're kickin' ass." Joe pulled two stacks of bills he'd shoved in his front pockets. "Must've taken in over five grand already."

Merle shook his head and ran across the street. The Anarchy Café was now taking up three times as much space as was legally permitted. The still-expanding right side had crushed a 1981 Pinto. There was blood on the cracked windshield.

As he walked back toward the Cafe, he wondered how long the outside would last until it outgrew the cheap black tarps they'd used to cover the exterior "walls."

He also wondered just how long they could keep this going until someone alerted the authorities that there was a gigantic dick expanding down South Main Street at an alarming rate.

"Excuse me," someone said as Merle was about to step inside.

Fuck, Merle thought.

"Do you work here?"

"Yes. Is there a problem?"

Before the tall fireman could speak, four naked people ran outside and pulled the city official into the club.

Merle ran after them, but the crazed partiers threw the fireman into the slam-dancing and raping crowd. As soon as the fireman landed on the floor, everyone turned toward him, their eyes glowing like the goat head's. The fireman was a big guy, but he was no match for the crowd, who held him down and took turns fucking him in the ass. The women shoved their pussies into his face and forced him to chow down.

"No!" Merle cried, but it was too late. When everyone had had their fill, the crowd ripped the fireman apart with their bare hands and threw the pieces into the air, where the moist ceiling seemed to absorb the offerings into its system. Its endless veins throbbed, causing the Café to expand yet again.

Shitshitshit. Merle ran to his office, realizing this venture had gone too far. But he quickly found out how wrong he was.

"You need to relax, brother." GG appeared in the office. Merle could still hear the band playing outside.

"Do you

know what just happened?"

"I said *relax.*"

The goat head spat a sticky substance into Merle's face. It tasted terrible, but once it slid down his throat, he began to unwind. He started thinking positively and forgot about the murder that had just occurred in his establishment. He forgot about the zoning laws they were violating, and he forgot about the potential lawsuits his raped customers could bring once this mass hysteria ended.

But he realized this *wasn't* mass hysteria. It was the Allin brothers' purpose. It had become their bread and butter and their reason for being.

* * *

Four months after the Anarchy Café opened, it had grown to half the size of New Hampshire. Patrons refused to leave, and just when Merle thought they'd have to force people out by any means necessary, the club would expand to accommodate not only the regulars, but also curiosity-seekers. Club kids and all sorts of nightlife types came from around the globe to get a glance inside the Anarchy Café. Some didn't survive the experience. Some did, and most of those who did became permanent fixtures.

By the fifth month, and with *three quarters* of New Hampshire now a gigantic penile nightclub, Merle and GG were approached by the United States military, as well as several men dressed in black suits with dark sunglasses. They were told things had gone off the rails and they needed to cut back.

GG dropped his pants to reveal the goat head, but its glowing eyes and psychic abilities had no effect on the government officials or the mysterious suits. And when the officials arrived back at the Anarchy Café the next day with a flatbed truck carrying a huge hypodermic needle, Merle saw GG's countenance sag.

"This is courtesy of Uncle Sam," one of the military officers said.

Two black helicopters lifted the needle from the truck, flew over the club, then dropped it tip-first onto the roof. GG watched in horror as the plunger depressed itself and filled the cock/club with a bubbling purple liquid. There must've been a swimming pool's worth of government medicine in there.

GG fell to the floor and screamed. When Merle tried to console him, GG involuntarily kicked him in the mouth, knocking out a few teeth. It took a couple hours, but the Anarchy Café slowly shrank back into GG's normal-sized cock. As it did, patrons who refused to leave were crushed to death, suffocating under the apocalyptic shrinkage. Plenty of people could've escaped, but it was as if the nightclub *owned* them. Both GG and Merle eventually agreed it had been one of the largest mass suicides in American history, although the media, for whatever reason, never picked up on what could've been a truly sensational story. Blood ran from the entrance, so deep that the military had to commission over a dozen septic tank trucks to park outside and suck everything up with their industrial-sized hoses.

Merle slammed his head against a telephone pole as he watched his brother's dick—and their newfound fortune—dwindle down to nothing.

* * *

Two weeks after the Anarchy Cafe's gruesome finale, Merle finally located a doctor in Manhattan who would be able to re-attach his brother's penis. The goat head had fallen off as soon as the nightclub was injected, and he was sick and tired of watching GG sticking his hand in the hole in his groin.

The operation was a success, although GG was now only four inches (even erect), due in large part to the months of abuse as an oversized nightclub and the effects of the mysterious military serum.

Upon their return to the mostly flattened New Hampshire, Merle and GG were arrested on several charges, including zoning law violations and endless property damage.

But Merle thought as positively as the now-lost goat head had encouraged. At least the time they'd spend in jail would be used writing their next several seven-inches, and maybe even a full album.

And he knew GG would be plotting a way to get even with Amanda.

THE BOWL

Author's Note: This story is my tribute/homage to Bentley Little, who since 1997 has been my favorite horror writer. I think the tale takes on a flavor of its own, but I tried to capture the sense of the macabre that Little is such an undisputed master of.

Harold Anderson stared out the bedroom window, restless thanks to his wife's snoring. The occasional bat fluttered by the street light, casting distorted shadows on his ceiling.

"Come on, honey," he said, pushing Helen onto her side.

She half-consciously rolled over and fell right back to sleep.

Although his plan worked, it was the silence that now kept him awake. He decided to watch a late re-run of the *Tonight Show*, but was still alert when it ended.

3:30 a.m.

He sat up, looking at the clothes he'd neatly laid out for tomorrow (today, actually). When he laid back down, his stomach gurgled loud enough to make Helen shift.

"Whoa," he said, rubbing his belly. "I shouldn't have had that second helping."

He stepped into his *#1 Dad* slippers (a Christmas gift from Danny), slid on his bathrobe (a birthday gift from Nadine), then padded toward the bathroom. With each step, the need to expel last night's dinner became more severe. Where had this come from? Four and a half hours of trying to fall asleep without so much as a fart, and now...

He reached into the darkness and felt for the switch. He dropped his robe as soon as the lime-colored bathroom was illuminated. The toilet—situated strategically between the sink and shower—seemed to beckon him. After pulling the latest issue of *Entertainment Weekly* from a magazine bin, Harold dropped his boxers and perched himself on the cool porcelain.

He read through the entire film review section before finishing his business. He broke the silence with two courtesy flushes along the way.

"That's the last time I let her talk me into Mexican on a work night," he said, washing his sweaty hands and face with lukewarm water. He put the robe back on, then gave the room a few cinnamon-scented blasts of Glade, making the place smell like a combo of Big Red Chewing Gum and ass.

He turned to walk back to bed. Someone said "thank you" in the blackened hallway.

Harold jumped. He flicked the bathroom lights back on, expecting to see Danny or Nadine up for a late-night pee. But on second thought, the voice was too *deep* for a five- or eight-year-old.

He checked his children's bedrooms, happy to see them both asleep.

Man, do I need some shut-eye. Harold turned off the bathroom light and scratched the top of his auburn head.

He crawled under the blankets next to Helen, and within five minutes joined her in slumberland.

* * *

"You look bushed! Tough time last night?" Mr. Davis asked.

"I had a bit of trouble falling asleep. My stomach did backflips for a while."

"Glad to see you're here—you know we have that meeting with Tucker right after lunch today?"

"That's why I'm here, even if I got less than three hours of sleep," Harold said, taking a swig from his third cup of coffee.

"That's the spirit!" Mr. Davis patted him on the back. "This is why you're my number one man."

At 11:43, Harold felt a sudden need to visit the restroom. He closed the file he was working on and headed to the lavatory.

He sat on the toilet, feeling disgusted by the prospect of doing this in a $600 suit. He experienced feelings of emptiness. Coldness. He couldn't wait to finish. His heart began racing, as if he was having a panic attack.

He soon felt relieved to be rid of whatever was inside him, and to be off the office toilet; just knowing two dozen people shared it gave him the willies.

"Mr. Anderson? Call on line one."

"Thank you, Margaret. I'll take it in my office."

"Please hold one moment," she said, smiling as Harold passed by.

"Hello, Harold Anderson here."

Silence.

"Hello, may I help you?"

Silence. Then, "Thank you."

"Excuse me?"

Silence. A rusty *click.* "Thank you."

Harold leaned forward in his plush leather chair. "I'm afraid I don't understand. Who is this?"

"You know who this is, and I know what you just did."

Harold slammed the phone down. "Freaking lunatic!"

Immediately, the phone rang in the lobby. He heard Margaret answer, then page him on the intercom. He accepted the call.

"Hello? Anderson here."

"If you ever hang up on me again, I'll destroy your wife and kids."

"Okay—who is this? What's your problem?"

Silence. Deafening, painful silence. Then the distinct sound of a toilet flushing. "Have a good day. We'll discuss this later."

"We'll discuss what later?"

The phone went dead.

The voice was familiar, but Harold couldn't match it to a face. He walked around his desk, anticipating another call.

It never came.

He left the office shortly after 5:00 p.m., still haunted by the menacing telephone conversation. Even the successful meeting with Tucker Industries couldn't keep his mind off that voice. He spent the forty-minute drive home trying to figure out who would first thank him for something, then threaten to kill his family in the next breath.

Must be a prank. Harold tuned into a classic rock station as he hit the highway.

* * *

He couldn't decide if it was the threat on his family or his lack of sleep, but something caused Harold to make love to his wife like a veteran porn star. She fell asleep right after their intense session, and hunger hit the thirty-seven-year-old film distributor like never before.

With eyes half-opened, Harold packed down a large bowl of Wheaties, adding sugar every five bites or so. The house was silent, and even Helen seemed to be resting snore-free.

Harold tossed the plastic bowl into the sink. As he began his trek back upstairs, a familiar urgency began building in his stomach.

He grabbed *Entertainment Weekly*, and scanned the book review section. He had eaten a light lunch and a sensible dinner, but he filled the toilet like a dump truck packing a new driveway with wet cement.

He closed both his eyes and the magazine, reaching behind himself to flush.

The tank forced down the waste, but did little to alleviate the stench. He thoroughly cleaned himself, and as always, blasted the room with Glade air freshener.

He made sure to wash his hands meticulously, then sprinkled some of the water onto his face and chest, wondering if this was yet another backlash from the Mexican feast.

"Thank you."

Harold spun around. "Who said that?"

Silence.

"Danny, if this is you breaking my chops, I'll punish you for a week!"

He walked across the hallway to find his son out cold. He even tickled Danny's foot to make sure he wasn't acting.

Harold stepped into his slippers as the voice came into his head loud and clear.

"Thank you, Harold. But please don't hang up on me like you did this afternoon…I found that to be most rude."

"W-who is this?" *What am I saying?* "Who—"

"It's me, Harold. Your only true friend in this world."

Harold scanned the bathroom, stuck his head back into the hallway, and even opened the small window in the shower. No one was outside, and as far as he could tell, no one was in the house.

Is this what lack of sleep does? Harold shut off the bathroom lights, spooked to the bone.

"I wasn't finished, Harold. Please come back in here."

"Please come in where?" he asked, his mind racing in all directions.

"In the bathroom. Where else do you expect me to be?"

Hands trembling, Harold switched the lights back on. The sink, shower, and toilet stood at attention, ready to be used by his waking family.

"I need you to help me with something, Harold."

Harold stood silent. Was this voice in his head, or was it audible to others? He didn't even consider waking Helen after the great time she provided this evening—not to mention, she'd laugh her head off if he tried to explain he was hearing voices in the bathroom.

"Who are you? How are you talking to me?"

"I need your help."

"Who—"

The toilet seat cover lifted itself up. Harold took a step back as the handle jiggled, causing a quick blast of blue dye to shoot into the water.

Oh my God.

"So, are you going to get over your amazement and listen to what I have to say?"

"Who are you—"

"Harold, I'm running out of patience. You may think I have all the time in the world, but there's more work for me to do than just take everyone's crap all day long—no pun intended."

Harold walked to the toilet. The seat snapped shut.

"Yes, dummy, it's me. Now listen—"

Harold slammed the door and took off down the hallway, then jumped down the stairs three at a time to the first floor. He leaned against the kitchen sink, both exhausted and horrified. He slid down and curled into the fetal position.

He still heard his toilet bowl's muffled voice carrying from upstairs.

"Harold," it said. "You're not making this easy on yourself, or on me. Now come back up here."

It took several minutes, but the combined elements of exhaustion and panic helped Harold slip into an uncomfortable sleep.

* * *

Harold awoke the next morning to his kids laughing and his wife poking him in the ribs.

"Honey, what are you doing down here?"

"Oh, man, what time is it?"

"Don't worry, you should be able to get in on time," Helen said, a smile forming on her face.

He looked up at the clock. "I came down for a snack and the next thing I knew, I couldn't keep my eyes open."

"Maybe you'd better take the day off and catch up on some sleep?"

"No can do. Not after landing the deal with Tucker yesterday," Harold said, kissing her on the cheek.

He hugged his kids, then headed upstairs to shower and dress.

He felt weird while shaving in the bathroom, expecting the toilet to start talking to him again. But it didn't. He picked up the phone next to the bowl (his wife insisted on it, since he spent so much time in there) and dialed Margaret at the office.

* * *

"I tried to be nice with you, Harold. I guess now I'll have to do things *my* way."

Harold was at his desk for less than a minute when the call came in. He gripped the receiver tightly, causing a hairline crack.

"Go about your day, Harold. I'll make *sure* Helen and the kids are properly looked after—"

"Now you listen to me, you son of a—"

Click.

Silence.

Not taking any chances, Harold dialed home. His wife answered on the second ring.

"Helen, are you okay?"

"Ummm—*yeah?* Why, what's wrong?"

What's wrong? Harold rubbed his forehead, wondering if he should have even called.

"Harry?"

"I'm sorry, hon. I guess you were right about me staying home today, but you know how Mr. Davis gets. Just do me a favor and watch yourself…keep an eye on the kids, too."

"That's it! Now tell me what's going on. I've never heard you acting this strange before."

Crap. "Nothing's going on, babe. I'm just feeling a little paranoid for some reason."

"*For some reason?* Harold Anderson, when you get home tonight, I'm forcing you into bed. You know you can be a real basket case when you don't get enough sleep."

"Yeah, you're right. I'll call you later."

"Okay. Maybe Mr. Davis will let you grab a nap at lunchtime."

"We'll see. I love you, hon."

"Love you too. Please try to take it easy."

As soon as he hung up, his boss stomped into his office.

"Anderson!" Mr. Davis said, a huge smile lighting up his face. "The Tucker people will be here tonight to seal the deal!"

"*Already?*"

"Yes!" He shook Harold's hand. "I need you to be present around seven-thirty this evening in the executive boardroom."

"Of course."

"Excellent. We're ordering Chinese around six. The usual?"

"Sure, the usual sounds fine."

Mr. Davis left, bragging to Margaret and laughing like he'd just won the lottery. Harold dialed Helen to tell her not to expect him until after 9:00.

* * *

Reeling from the excitement of landing one of his career's biggest deals, Harold turned off the highway. Helen would be thrilled when she saw the size of his commission.

Helen.

Harold realized he'd forgotten to call her during lunch or dinner, and hoped she wouldn't be standing at the front door fuming; if there was one thing Helen Anderson required, it was that he stayed in touch throughout the day. Harold never questioned this, and in fact liked to hear his wife's voice as often as possible; even their closest friends admired their commitment to each other.

The dashboard clock read 9:42 when Harold pulled into the driveway. The house was dark, except for the light coming from Danny's room and the upstairs bathroom.

"I'm home," Harold said, slinging his suit jacket over a kitchen chair. Although the kids were usually getting ready for bed at this time, Helen rarely—if ever—went upstairs until after 11:00.

"He-ll-ooooo?"

When no one answered, Harold started feeling nervous. Panic returned. *I'll destroy your wife and kids.* As a precaution, he grabbed the largest knife from a block on the counter, then slowly ascended the stairs.

Danny's door was open. Harold carefully peeked inside, then dropped the knife onto the carpet.

His son and daughter kneeled on the floor, putting the finishing touches on astonishingly detailed Play-Doh toilets.

"W-what are you guys doing?"

"Hi, Daddy," Nadine said, her eyes still glued to her work. "Aren't these beautiful?"

"Hey, Dad. Do we have any more Play-Doh downstairs?"

Each sculpture was at least a foot tall, multi-colored, and crafted beyond either of his children's natural talents.

"Why are you guys making toilet bowls?"

"Silly daddy! They aren't toilet bowls—"

"They're statues of our master," Danny said, remaining focused on his work.

Harold's mind shifted from panic to rage. "Where's your mother?"

Neither child answered. Harold stepped in the room and grabbed Danny by the back of his shirt. "I asked you a question, young man. I asked you where your mother is."

"We can't be bothered answering such petty questions, Dad. Don't you know we must complete this before the master is angered?"

Danny's eyes looked cloudy, in need of a pint of Visine. Harold left him with Nadine and ran to his bedroom. The bed was in shambles, but Helen was nowhere to be found.

"She's with me, Harold."

That voice. Harold dashed to the bathroom and kicked in the door.

His wife was on her knees before the toilet bowl, kissing the seat. Harold could tell the room had been recently cleaned, due to the strong smell of Lysol.

"Helen! What are you doing?"

"Let her be, Harold. I told you I would destroy your wife and kids if you disrespected me again. But I've taken a liking to them, especially to your wife. They can all be *very* useful to me."

This is insane! How can the toilet…am I losing my mind? Am I awake?

"Yes, Harold. I *am* talking to you, and you're not losing your mind. However, I am losing patience with *you.* I called you five times at work this afternoon and you never answered."

Helen licked the entire seat, then hugged the tank, passionately kissing the flush handle. She wore the red see-through nightie Harold had bought her last Valentine's Day.

"Helen! Stop it!" Harold ran over to pull his wife off the toilet.

The seat opened and sucked her face into the water before slamming down on her neck. The bowl began flushing frantically, the seat so tight

Harold couldn't pull her away. He wrapped his arms around her waist and tugged with everything he had.

But within two minutes, Helen's body went limp. The seat raised itself and she slid to the floor, her face blue and soulless, her neck visibly snapped.

Harold took the heavy lid off the tank and raised it over his head.

"You don't want to do that, Harold. I haven't told you what I need from you—"

Frenzied, Harold smashed the toilet bowl into countless pieces, chunks of porcelain flying across the bathroom and over his wife's corpse.

The voice finally stopped.

"No, daddy! We need to finish this!" Nadine said.

Harold tucked his daughter under his arm, then dragged Danny by the shirt, ignoring their kicking and screaming. He couldn't believe how his children had rebelled and gave their allegiance to the fiendish fixture. He tried as hard as he could to believe Helen wasn't really gone.

He had to duct-tape his children's hands behind their backs before putting them in the car. They screamed as he drove off.

Danny slammed his head against the window in the back seat.

"He'll punish us, dad! Don't you understand?"

"He won't be punishing anyone anymore, Danny," Harold said, looking over his shoulder as if making sure the bowl hadn't reconstructed itself and somehow followed them.

"WHAT? What have you done to him?" Nadine said, tears running over her tiny cheeks. "WHAT HAVE YOU DONE TO HIM?"

When Harold pulled to the end of the street, Greg Hammond ran in front of the car with a small sledgehammer.

"Harold!" he yelled through the window. "Are you okay?"

"All considering...what are you doing with that thing?"

"I think you know, judging by the look on your face." Greg quickly lit a cigarette. "I smashed almost everyone on our block."

Harold rolled down his window.

"It's everywhere, Harry! Everywhere in this area, anyway. They're taking over! We gotta destroy them while we can!"

"Where's everyone else?"

"You, me, and your kids are the only ones left around here, as far as I can tell."

Harold was so taken by the news, he didn't realize Greg was running back toward his garage. "Where are you going?"

"I'll be right back—wait for me!"

Harold tried tuning into the pre-set news radio stations, but the only thing being broadcasted was the sound of flushing toilets and commercials for various bathroom cleaners.

Greg came back with another sledgehammer. "Are you ready?"

"Let's do it."

Harold parked on the next block. In the middle of the street stood a burly-looking man with a cinder block, waving them on.

They emerged from Harold's car, both children still screaming in the back seat, then walked up to their unknown neighbor.

"Gentlemen," he said in a burly voice. "Looks like we have our work cut out for us."

Harold and Greg nodded, then followed him into the first house.

HERS IS A LUSH SITUATION

Author's Note: One of the many novels I started writing was titled CANDY WASHINGTON: BITCH OF THE LIVING DEAD. But, alas, the zombie genre had become beyond played out, so it went on the back burner. I re-worked (make that heavily re-worked) the first chapter when a call went out for an anthology about queefs. If you don't know what a queef/quif is, please consult Google or your preferred Internet search engine. I think this is one of the more unusual anthologies out there. I did a live reading of this story at a convention and it went over very well. I named it after a really weird Bill Nelson song, which was playing as I wrote the final draft.

I knew I'd never trust another person the night Sister Margaret tried to lick my pussy. That was at St. John's Academy, an allegedly upper-class establishment where, along with academics, child rape was a common interest among the faculty. Although I was just seven years old at the time, I managed to convince some crying girl stuck with me in detention to help me get back at that old dyke, but neither of us thought it would've ended with St. John's burned to the ground and

Sister Margaret's demise…or with my mom and her jerk-off boyfriend disowning me (which, as far as I'm concerned, happened the moment they informed me I'd been signed up for boarding school).

But you know what?

Fuck 'em.

Fuck 'em both.

Fuck all of 'em.

Any nun who tries to shove her pudgy cheeks between the legs of a seven year old deserves to have a match thrown on her—and if even *half* of what we were taught in religion class was true, the bitch is still burning today. And my "parents" would soon join her.

Good.

The ten years of juvie were worth it. Yeah, the assholes running *that* place were no better than the priests and nuns at St. John's, but at least they didn't throw you into detention when you tried to fight back. Sure, they'd kick your ass and party it twice as hard, but it was nice going to sleep afterwards knowing the warden had a bloody bite mark on her floppy tit, or one of her limp-dicked guards wouldn't be walking for a week.

My early teenage years had dissolved by the time I was released from Rockford Juvenile Detention Center, along with any remaining interest I had left for the human race. This is probably the reason I'm still surviving today, five years after I was let out.

I managed to get a job as a bartender's helper at a dive called Roy's Tavern on the Lower East Side. I brought up cases of beer from the rat-infested cellar, occasionally wiping off the four tables that decorated the space. Although I was paid crap money, Roy let me live with him for free.

Of course, nothing's really *free*, but blowing the old bastard once in a while was nothing compared to where I'd been and what I'd done—most of the time against my will. I had it made with Roy, and within a few weeks I was making more money giving hand-jobs in the bathroom than the tavern pulled in on a typical night. Amazing how easy it was to make money like this, especially after the assholes had a few beers in them.

Roy busted me yanking off some out-of-place yuppie one night (hey—a hundred bucks is a hundred bucks), but instead of firing me or even getting mad, he went back up front and continued drying the whiskey glasses, an impressive feat for a man/yak hybrid whose hands consisted of three fingers and two parts of a hoof.

Yeah. *A lot* had changed while I was being punished for sticking up for myself.

"I'm—"

"Shhh," he'd said.

Funny how we communicated. I surprised myself that night for *almost* apologizing to someone, but he'd cut me off before I could.

Roy was like that. I even offered to give him a cut of the profits, but he refused. I'd shared my life story with him the first night we fucked, and didn't need to say anymore. My love for the hairy bastard grew every day.

He never asked for another blowjob after the yuppie incident, but on nights when I could tell he had it rough, I'd go down on him anyway.

Roy was like the dad I never knew.

A couple of jerk-offs came into the bar one night, looking for a good time; apparently word was getting out that the new chick at Roy's was taking care of men in the bathroom for a decent fee. I must admit, though, that overhearing one of those guys say, "That must be her—man, she *is* hot!" made me feel good after years of that fat piece-of-shit warden calling me an ugly skank-ho before pissing on my face.

They both wanted to be taken care of at the same time, but I said they'd have to take turns, and they reluctantly agreed after turning and whispering something to each other.

I hardly had the first asshole's dick out of his pants when his buddy walked in on us and had his embarrassingly small cock out and ready for action. I wasn't scared of these over-groomed clowns, just really pissed off realizing they'd probably had this planned.

I played it cool. "Come here," I said to the second idiot, and he walked over like a mermaid as his pants dropped. "Let's get this over with."

I started to work both guys with my hands. Their silly smirks pissed me off even more than the fact that they'd disobeyed my rules. I decided to mess with them when I could feel one was about to blow.

"I thought I said no two-at-a-time?"

"Fuckin' bitch," asshole number two said as I stopped stroking him. "Keep going!"

I kept at it...but only on his friend, who was small, too, but not embarrassingly so. Asshole number two realized I was done with him and finished himself off, hitting his friend in the leg.

"Come on, bro! What's wrong with you?"

Realizing what he did, asshole number two said, looking at me, "This is *your* fault, you filthy—"

The next thing I knew, asshole number two was out cold on the damp, sticky floor. Asshole number one—that's what I ended up calling him, even though he seemed nicer than his friend—slammed into the floor, too, although I didn't get to finish him.

"'You okay?" Roy asked. He stood behind both unconscious assholes with his Louisville Slugger fitted awkwardly in his hand/hooves. I had seen the bat stashed behind the bar, but this was the first time I'd seen it in action.

"Yeah. Thanks," I said, walking over to the sink, the warm water flushing the two assholes' funk from my hands. "How did—"

—*you know?* I was about to ask, before I caught myself and realized that Roy *was*, at this point, my father, my protector, my boss...and my occasional lover.

I eventually learned that Roy knew *everything* that went down in his place, and he had evidently overheard my bar-side conversation with the two assholes. I dried my hands, then threw them around Roy's neck, kissing his scruffy but comforting cheek, the only part of his body not covered in hair. "You're my angel, Roy."

As I kissed him, he wrapped his arm around my waist and gave me a soft, reassuring squeeze.

I'm still not sure if it was Roy's hug or my own happiness over being stood up for, but I felt a puff of air escape from between my legs. It made a sound that let Roy know it had come from the front. I thought he would be turned off, but he smiled as he kissed me back on my cheek and then leaned his bat against the sink.

We each took an asshole by the foot and dragged them out the back door. Roy reached into one guy's pulled-down pants and took his wallet. He handed it to me, then I followed him back inside the bar. Considering the coffee shop a few doors down had just taken their trash out, I had the feeling that the two assholes would be woken up by rats if some homeless bum didn't pee on them first.

After the five new customers were taken care of, I sat at the end of the bar and thumbed through the asshole's wallet. $460 in twenties; I assumed they hadn't planned on spending this much for two handjobs. I divided the money, and when Roy eventually went to take a leak, I tucked $230.00 in the register, knowing he wouldn't take it if I handed it to him.

Ten minutes after he returned, I was clearing one of the tables when I felt something enter my back pocket. Roy winked and walked back to the bar. He'd make a terrible pickpocket with those hand-hooves.

Bastard. He didn't want any of the money, so I left it at that. It felt good to have so much cash on me.

Stanley left around a quarter to three. He was one of Roy's regulars, although this was the first time we saw him on a Tuesday night (or Wednesday morning, if you want to get technical). I had already finished my cleaning routine. Roy was out back, checking on the status of the two assholes.

"They're gone," I remember him saying when he came back in. "Probably had no clue where they were." He chuckled and looked out the front window, then at me.

We locked the place up and walked four blocks to Roy's—make that *our* apartment—and fell asleep before 4:30. I guess the whole thing with the two assholes had worn us out more than we realized. Roy had fallen asleep with his arm around my waist, and despite me being tired from everything that went down, I found myself aroused when—in his sleep—he tightened his hug and forced another blast of air from my front. But I fell asleep knowing I'd get the old man to take care of me before we got up for breakfast.

THE LIFE MACHINE

(or, How the Boardwalk Tried to Darken the World)

Author's Note: This one was inspired by an actual event that took place at Seaside Heights in New Jersey. I was trying to play on the Drumscape machine (an electronic drum set where you can play along to various songs) in an arcade, when some guy who was obviously a bit too zealous started pressuring me to hurry up so he could get on it. I sat on a bench across the boardwalk and watched him play for a bunch of people as I sipped a beer and planned out the following tale. I often wonder if the guy killed himself when I returned the following summer and discovered Drumscape had been removed…

I had to dog-ear the paperback when a dissident gray cloud refused to move on. I'd spent the last hour immersed in an interesting thriller, the pages illuminated by a ninety-five-degree August sun. My kids frolicked in the surf while my wife conversed with a few other moms we'd met earlier back at the motel.

The scent of freshly-grilled sausage drifted on the wind, followed by the serene sounds of the shore: flip-flops slapped bare heels, game attendants fished for players, and various types of music pumped through the booths, stands and restaurants lined up and down the seaside.

I tucked my book into the towel/sunscreen/various-other-ointments bag and headed for the boardwalk, my wife probably figuring I had to use the restroom. The kids continued playing, oblivious to anything around them.

The outdoor shower was ice-cold, but it rinsed the sand off my feet. It felt good to be back in socks and sneakers. I wiped the dust from my sunglasses as I stepped up on the vast wooden walkway. I strolled by an arcade, a pizza place and a psychic reader. A fresh lemonade stand tempted me to part with $2.00, but it didn't tempt me as much as the young long-haired brunette licking a vanilla cone, pretending to be comfortable in the customized dental floss she wore as a bathing suit.

I noticed a few more gray clouds moving in from the south, bullying the white ones. Several people on the beach began packing up their things. In the distance, two men in wetsuits raced each other to shore on surfboards. I visualized a giant shark swallowing them whole just before they reached land—a brief, realistic panic, then my attention was re-focused on another arcade I hadn't noticed before.

You'd think after five days in the same vacation spot and at least fifty walks up and down the same boardwalk, you'd be familiar with all the attractions.

I squinted as a blast of sunshine reached my face through the darkening skies: Bonzo's Game Room.

How'd I miss this one?

I checked my pockets for quarters—there were several—then entered the air-conditioned room.

Skee-Ball. Pinball. A few of the newer "shoot-the-terrorist/zombie" games. I began to lose hope when I finally saw a beautiful, original *Asteroids* machine standing behind a pole, close to where I had entered.

Surprisingly, all the control buttons worked. I was having a great time destroying space rocks generated by ancient computer graphics when I noticed everything outside had turned black.

I rushed to the door—with two more ships to my credit—and fell silent. The boardwalk had been vacated. I ran to the edge of the walkway, looking in horror as I saw the beach littered with towels and bathing suits. The lifeguard seat was empty except for a whistle and a pair of sunglasses.

I froze, wondering if I had died, or if something sinister had happened during the few moments I played the videogame. When no choking or burning sensations came, I figured I was safe, then remembered there was an old man working the change counter inside Bonzo's Game Room.

I turned around and spotted him behind the counter. Even from that distance, I saw tears in his eyes, and realized the arcade must've been some kind of haven, but had I forfeited its protection since stepping outside?

I ran back in. I whipped by the *Asteroids* machine (which was now playing the frantic sounds of a UFO attack), almost tripped on a step-up box for short people, then reached the change/prize redemption counter unscratched.

"Excuse me, do you know what's going on out there?" I asked.

The old man stared straight ahead, answering without making eye contact. "He hasn't been here today." A tear rolled over his plump left cheek, spilling onto the glass countertop.

"Who is *he*?"

The old man swallowed hard, then walked around the counter, taking me by the wrist. "Do you hear that?"

I heard nothing but the muffled sound of waves hitting the shore.

"That's the sound of silence…because he hasn't come."

I was about to ask again who this *he* was when the old man walked me to the front of the arcade. The *Asteroids* screen dimmed (like everything else in the place), and outside seemed to grow darker. I probably would've gasped if not for the cool, conditioned air of Bonzo's.

"He hasn't come," the old man said for the third time, pointing at an unusual machine. He motioned for me to go inside, and I obeyed out of pure fear.

I walked to the black machine, which was the size of an old-fashioned dunking booth. I looked inside the rear window to see an electric drum set, a pair of wood sticks tied to a rope, and a small stool. A red-lighted slot stated "4 x .25 to play." Apparently it was some kind of musical game.

"He hasn't come today. The music's leaving. The silence is coming."

The old man began melting into the filthy, paper-thin carpet. A bunch of green and blue tentacle-type things appeared on the floor in a glowing mist, wrapped around his shoulders and pulled him down. I vaguely heard him say "…rums…" as his melting features were swallowed.

The front of the arcade—all glass doors facing the boardwalk—shattered. I covered my head and ran back outside as the shards flew inward.

Although it was no later than 2:00 p.m., the sky was blacker than midnight, not a single light as far as I could see. The silence started to terrify me; the waves continued crashing, but I heard nothing. A pain grew in my stomach as I thought about my family, wondering if they were in the same place as the old man and the rest of the vacationers.

Drops of rain hit my face and arms. The liquid was red, reminding me of blood; but I knew it wasn't, because blood wasn't this cold or transparent.

Despair started setting in. I crouched down on my knees, praying, fighting back tears, waiting for those ugly appendages to come and pull me down—

—I noticed something happening inside the drum machine. Wings flapped. Tentacles swung up from below. I stood cautiously, trying to discern the incident.

Two seagulls, their bodies stained pink from the rain, flew toward me, each one carrying a drumstick in its beak. An eerie glow followed them across the boardwalk, tentacles violently lashing upwards, trying to pull them back.

But the gulls were too quick.

They dropped the sticks into my soaked hands. The glow and the tentacles stopped advancing, but remained where they were.

"You know what to do," one of the seagulls said.

"Don't let us down. We think they finally got *him*."

I stared at the birds as the tentacles snatched them in mid-air. As one was pulled under the boardwalk, it screamed, "Now it's up to *you*."

The air got darker.

The only visible light flowed from the electronic drumming booth. I dashed forward, expecting to be pulled down by the disgusting feelers. But I made it safely, then searched my saturated pants for quarters. I sat on the tiny stool and jammed coins into the machine like a paramedic administering antivenin to a snakebite victim. A mechanical voice was amplified.

Choose Level. Tap any pad to select.

I banged the snare drum quickly and selected "concert master" over "beginner." I was no wizard, but I had held my own in a few bands when I was just out of high school.

Choose song.

An enormous list flashed across the screen: '70s rock, '80s rock and metal, '90s alternative, classic rock, modern rock, punk rock, hip-hop, country. A few more styles popped up, but I paid them no mind as I tapped the snare to select *punk rock*.

The list was disappointing; mostly newer bands I'd never heard of. Where were the Clash and the Sex Pistols and the Damned and the Ramones? I selected Bad Religion and played along to one of their slower songs, which I vaguely remembered from the end of my "hang-out" days. I heard the boardwalk creaking behind me. I searched for a volume control, but there was none.

By the time the song ended, my arms were a bit sore. I hadn't played in almost twenty years, let alone to a song I barely knew. A tentacle started slipping through the side window, but retracted when I selected another song—the machine didn't ask for additional quarters.

I switched over to *classic rock* and began pulverizing the rubber pads to Edgar Winter's "Frankenstein," one of my favorite warm-up songs. I saw the boardwalk and beach reflected behind me on the green-tinted monitor. Tentacles were springing up between the boards, maniacally thrashing about, their color more gruesome between the colored rain and its translation on the screen.

The old man's head stuck out of the floor between my legs. "Good going, kid. Keep it up—" and then he was dragged back under. I smiled at the idea of being called a kid at thirty-eight years of age, then wondered what kind of battle was going on underneath the boardwalk; whatever kind, it was a battle in which I had become a crucial participant.

Choose song.

The mechanical voice seemed to plead with me to hurry up and decide. I tapped the snare, landing on '80s rock and metal.

Before the tentacle could enter the window again, "Bark at the Moon" blared through the speakers, and out of instinct I knew when to hit all the opening chops. I knew the song, but had never played it before.

"Yeah! That's it, baby! Rock 'n' roll!" The face and arms of a balding (but still long-haired) man came out of the boardwalk behind me, his head banging against the wood and his hands making devil horn signs. Glowing mist surrounded him, but the more I played, the more he came out of the wood. During the guitar solo, the dental floss was now standing up, the brunette's curvy figure slowly filling it out. Her head also swung up and down in time to my beat. The skies were still black and the red rain still poured, making her face look like Carrie at the prom.

As I tried to concentrate on my playing, I couldn't help but notice—

through the reflection in the monitor—all kinds of unrelated objects flopping in and out of the water, some making it onto the sand and burrowing like groundhogs—toasters that seemed to be made of flesh; oversized ashtrays; oversized produce; oversized Patrolmen's Benevolent Association cards; rotary phones with no dial numbers; a seemingly endless parade of rooks from Civil War chess sets. Finally, a massive herd of cheap K-Mart guitars slammed down into the sand, causing sounds underneath the boardwalk that tried to disrupt my playing.

But they didn't.

By the time the song ended, several people had gathered behind me. I could tell they were fans of metal music by their hairstyles and clothing.

Choose song.

I went to select another Ozzy track, figuring its power had somehow brought these people back from the abyss, when—

"Dude, we're all good. You have to get us all out." The balding man placed his hand on my shoulder.

"Please, don't stop. My brother and my boyfriend are down there," said dental floss girl, trying to keep warm as the rain pelted her 99% naked body. She held one of the flesh-looking toasters between her breasts; it seemed to radiate heat.

I selected a hip-hop song, figuring the beat couldn't be too difficult to follow.

It wasn't.

And by the time the old Public Enemy track ended, the crowd behind me had grown, this time with wanna-be gangstas and younger kids with baggy pants and loud jewelry. They cheered me on too, encouraging me to keep jamming to different music.

One of the seagulls flew into the machine and perched on my shoulder. "You're doing great—but don't stop."

I ran down the list of genres, doing my best to play the songs I didn't know, impressing myself with others that I hadn't heard or played in many years. The boardwalk was soon packed with people. The rain began letting up. The skies, while still dark, threatened the blackness with a clearer blue.

After two hours I was gasping for air, but I jammed on.

"Okay," the gull said, wiping sweat from my forehead with its wing. "There's one more style to go."

Without reading the last choice, I knew it was country.

I hated country.

I looked at the monitor and saw those two guys surfing again, my kids digging in the sand and my wife chatting with the other moms as if nothing had ever happened. A few people behind me cried, looking around for their loved ones.

I had to do this.

Against everything in my system, I jammed along to Garth Brooks and Toby Keith and Gretchen Wilson and the Dixie Chicks...but when I got to the last choice, Charlie Daniels, the skies immediately cleared up. I'd hardly begun his '70s hit "The Devil Went Down to Georgia" when I saw people hugging, teary eyes wiped clean, all remnants of the glowing mist dissolving back into the boardwalk. Dental Floss even stuck in her head and kissed me on the cheek as thanks for returning her boyfriend to her. Who would've imagined a metalhead and a country fan as an item?

My arms were exhausted. I stood up for a second to stretch my legs when the old man pushed me back onto the stool.

"Whoa...what do you think you're doing?"

"What? I'm getting some blood into my legs—"

"Never mind that. Look," he said, pointing to a renegade gray cloud drifting in from the south. He stuck his hand on top of the machine and gave me fifty credits.

Without saying a word, I began playing through the selections again. The cloud went away. The vacationers laughed and ate, played video games and Skee-Ball. Occasionally a small crowd gathered behind me to applaud and say thanks.

By midnight I was so tired I thought my arms would fall off. I saw my wife and kids walk back to the motel room carrying their towels and some stuffed animals they must've won at another arcade. I was dying for a slice of pizza or a nice sausage hero.

One of the gulls flew into the booth a few minutes after I desired these things and fed me a large mushroom slice with crushed red pepper.

The old man was taking coins from the machines, dumping out ashtrays, and preparing to lock up for the night. The power to the drum machine had finally been cut.

"You'll be back tomorrow?"

His eyes reminded me of a lost and beaten puppy who had lost its master. I thought of the tentacles, the glowing mist, the red rain and the skies that had turned so dark. The two seagulls sat atop the machine, apparently waiting for my reply.

"Do I have a choice?"

His smile almost cracked his glasses. "Great! See you at noon."

My family was gone when I got back to the motel room. I called my wife's cell from the office telephone. A message said: *Do what you have to do. We love you and we'll see you next summer.*

My heart broke.

But my obligation was clear.

I was now *him*.

I fell asleep on a boardwalk bench that night, trying to enjoy the last week of summer's warm weather, thinking about my kids and my wife and the boardwalk that tried to darken the world.

NICK CATO is the author of DON OF THE DEAD, THE APOCALYPSE OF PETER, THE LAST PORNO THEATER, THE ATROCITY VENDOR, UPTOWN DEATH SQUAD, and DEATH WITCH. His debut non-fiction film book, SUBURBAN GRINDHOUSE, will be released in late 2019. He has edited the anthologies DARK JESTERS (with co-editor LL Soares) and THE GRUESOME TENSOME: A SHORT STORY TRIBUTE TO THE FILMS OF HERSCHELL GORDON LEWIS. Nick has had fiction published in many anthologies and websites, and writes a film column for the recently revamped DEEP RED magazine.

Nick also oversees things at the long running fanzine/website THE HORROR FICTION REVIEW and hosts the SUBURBAN GRINDHOUSE podcast when he's not walking his two dachshunds.

www.ingramcontent.com/pod-product-compliance
Lightning Source LLC
LaVergne TN
LVHW091003080826
845145LV00003B/1106

* 9 7 8 1 9 4 7 6 5 4 8 5 3 *